Crow's Nest

Clive Willetts

First edition 2023
Published by Clive Willetts
Web: www.clive-willetts.com
Email: info@clive-willetts.com

ISBN: 978 1 7394768 0 9

Printed by: Direct2Print Stourbridge

Acknowledgements

With grateful thanks to:
Jane H
Chris P
Richard K
Derek A
Yvonne S
Ian R
Diane H

With special thanks to:
Mandy W
Miranda I
Dan P
Chris S
Barbara S

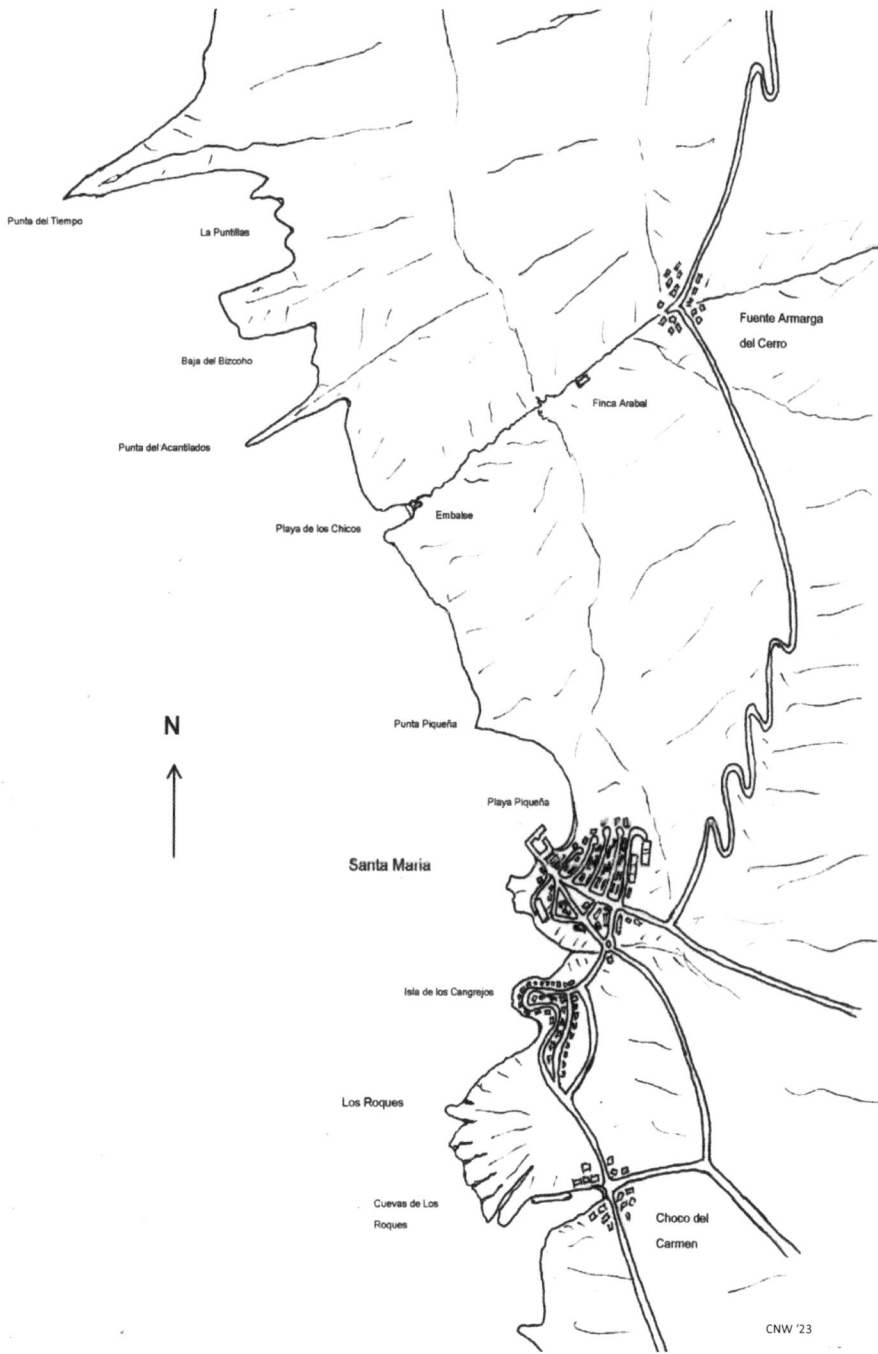

Punta del Tiempo

La Puntillas

Baja del Bizcoho

Punta del Acantilados

Playa de los Chicos

Embalse

Finca Arabal

Fuente Armarga
del Cerro

N
↑

Punta Piqueña

Playa Piqueña

Santa María

Isla de los Cangrejos

Los Roques

Cuevas de Los
Roques

Choco del
Carmen

CNW '23

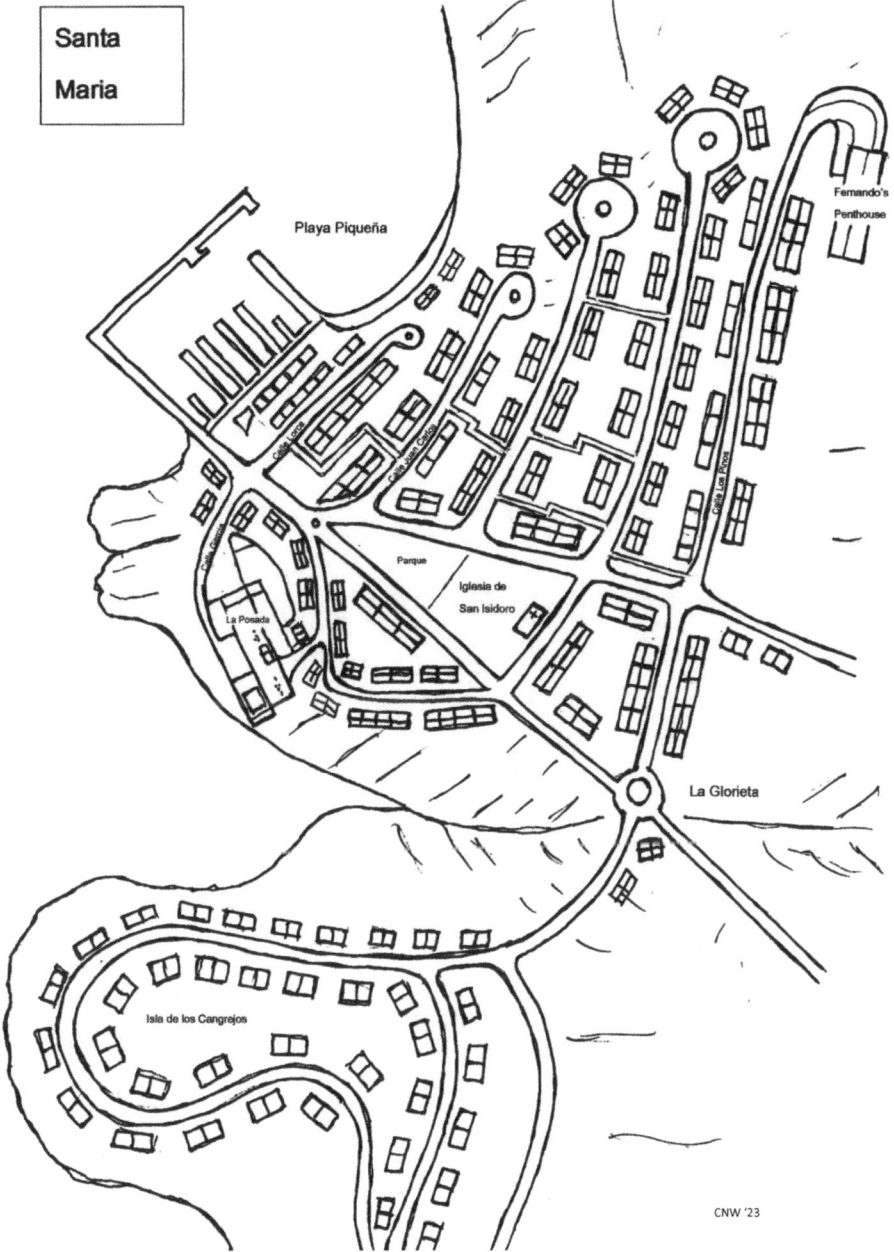

Santa Maria

Playa Piqueña

Fernando's Penthouse

Calle Lecla

Calle Juan Carlos

Calle Los Arcos

Calle Garcia

Parque

Iglesia de San Isidoro

La Posada

La Glorieta

Isla de los Cangrejos

CNW '23

PART 1

A runner donned in T-shirt, shorts and trainers, exited the building and jogged his way across the road. The sun had not yet arisen over the hills but he could see and hear signs of life in the town around him. His running was not fast, more of a gentle lope, as he trod his familiar route. His breathing was easy and he adjusted his cadence to suit each street and alleyway, incline and steps. He had no need for a watch or any other time-telling device for as he approached the town square, he could see the street light which housed a digital display: 01:01:1998, 8:30a.m., 16°c.

Zigzagging his way through the town, inexorably down towards the marina, he could feel his heartbeat strengthen in his chest but not from exertion. Taking the last few metres even more slowly as he advanced to the harbour, he was relieved to see no activity save for a lone fishing boat making its way towards the harbour mouth. Rounding the corner to his right he slowed to a stroll along the quayside, glancing from there to the buildings on his right. He slipped into a small passage and dropped down behind an air-conditioning unit. His view of the incoming boat was marred slightly but he watched it sail in and moor on the far quay.

He observed a pale yellow van drive down to the boat and the catch being unloaded when a small sound behind him made him stand and wheel around. The sun had now risen and was in his eyes but he could see that he was confronted by two men who bore down on him. He sidestepped the air-conditioner and backed out of the alleyway. Suddenly the nearest man rushed forward with both arms extended before him. The jogger felt the force of the full bodyweight of his assailant shoving him backwards at a speed he could not counter, he lost his balance and the sky came into view as he tumbled back, the rear of his head smashed into the concrete of the quayside, then oblivion.

*

1

Chapter 1 (Thurs 1/Jan/98)

Fernando Fernández, was a tall but slightly portly middle-aged financial adviser, and had risen early from his slumber. The view from his penthouse apartment was to the west and as he sat on his balcony terrace enjoying coffee, he watched the town and marina in the pre-dawn light. Soon it would be bathed in early morning brightness as the sun rose over the hills behind him and lit the blue Atlantic Ocean that shimmered in the distance.

It was the First of January 1998 and, despite having had a late night watching the stupendous fireworks display on the harbour below, he felt renewed and optimistic, ready for the New Year to come.

Leaving his coffee on the table, Fernando went to his kitchen to prepare a breakfast of bread, ham and cheese *bocadillo*, and then returned to the balcony. He could see the outline of the neighbouring island of La Goma and small fishing vessels, mobbed by expectant gulls, as they plied their way back to the harbour, where there was very little activity as it was too early for the paying public to board whale and dolphin watching boats.

He enjoyed his lofty position; like a sailor of old in his very own crow's nest; his apartment being the highest of all the dwellings climbing up the cliffs, overlooking his home town of Santa Maria.

On such a glorious morning, he felt sad that he had no one with which to share it. Having been widowed two years before, he was now more than a little lonely but at least he had his two sons, though they were far away, Miguel in Argentina and Pablo in California, thus adding to his solitude. Fernando did not mind his own company; he was quite productive by himself, nevertheless he still had to rely on his assistant Simon for the day-to-day running of his business.

*

Fernando had never been an outgoing man. He had a happy childhood, but his intellect and love of tidiness distanced him from his peers. The fact that he had no interest in sports also contributed to his introversion. Whilst his fellow students, at school and university, were full of pop music, football and general high jinks, he preferred Jazz, Classical music and cryptic crossword puzzles; he was reserved and studious.

With a dream of becoming a high-ranking Police officer, he had attended the National Police Academy (ENP - *Escuela Nacional de Policía*) near Madrid. However, during his second year, with advice from his tutors and Cristobal Dorantes, an experienced visitor lecturing on Anti-crime Services, they decided that forensic accountancy would be a better match for Fernando's skills. It was the start of a long friendship with Cristobal and they maintained close contact.

Fernando passed all of his examinations at the highest grade. Nevertheless, he still did not feel that he was on quite the right career path and decided to sidestep into tax advice and wealth management. Subsequently, at the age of twenty-five, he left the Police School and found a position with a prestigious firm of financial advisers. He stayed there for a year before opening an office of his own in La Joya.

However, his existence was bland. So in 1972 when Amanda came into his life, it was like the curtains had been drawn back and the windows flung wide open on a sunny springtime morning; light and love flooded into his life and new possibilities abounded.

He had received an invitation to attend an art exhibition, not his usual idea of an entertaining evening, but it was soon after opening his office and a gift from his very first client. Mainly abstract paintings but also some pencil drawings; he found the artwork was more interesting than he had expected, but when he was approached by a striking young lady with bubbly black hair, he forgot all about the exposition!

'Good evening, I'm Amanda de La Vega your host for this evening's presentation. Are you familiar with the artist's work?' she asked.

'I... um, not really, I just came along as I have this invitation...' Fernando offered his card.

'Ah, Señor Fernández, I see. Well, let me show you around.'

'Please Señorita, call me Fernando.'

'Only if you call me Amanda,' she said with a smile, glancing back over her shoulder at him as she turned to lead him away, and he was smitten.

3

She later confessed to her friends that she had fallen for him too, that same night, 'I saw a tall, young, handsome man, confident but with an air of mystery, and I simply had to know more about him.'

However, Amanda *was* gregarious and she had brought that with her into their marriage. Soon after, when their sons came along, Fernando found more and more, that a social life can have its benefits, for example; meeting with other parents and, of course, the prospective business that they could bring with them!

They had a blissful few years living on the outskirts of La Joya, Miguel and Pablo attended the local schools and later university. Fernando had taken on staff in his office and Amanda was managing the prestigious *Galería de la Islas* art gallery. Life was good.

In early 1994, Miguel was finishing his Degree and Pablo had started his, when their mother began to feel depressed. She was sick at some point almost daily for some weeks and quite tearful at times, but fought to keep it from her family.

She spoke with her doctor but he was at a loss and could only prescribe drugs to alleviate the symptoms, as there was no obvious cause for her distress.

Struggling on for several months, one morning when she had finished showering, she called Fernando into the bathroom.

'Look here,' she said, 'there's a small dimple on my left breast...' and I think that I can feel a lump...'

'It's probably nothing to worry about *amorcita*, it may be just a cyst,' Fernando said, reassuringly, 'but I'll contact the clinic straight away and get you examined.'

Fernando managed to get an appointment for her the following day and the doctor was displeased with what he found. He immediately called the hospital and was successful in getting Amanda seen that same day.

The breast specialist was not happy with Amanda's presentation either and performed a needle biopsy, the results of which were ready a week later.

4

Fernando and Amanda kept the condition from their boys who were distracted with their studies anyway. There was no need to worry them unnecessarily, but a stressful few days passed.

When she was called to the hospital to see the specialist, the results were devastating; it was cancer. She would need to have a full mastectomy, at the very least.

Just a week later, she was ready for surgery. Fernando helped her into her theatre gown and they were visited at the bedside by the surgeon, nurses, anaesthetist and hospital administrators. It was pitiful to see Amanda thus; her bouts of uncontrolled tears, the overwhelming desire to be somewhere else - anywhere else - crying and pleading to be spared from the situation she was in.

Thankfully, the pre-medication began to take effect and, lying on the bed, she drifted off to sleep, but she awoke when the theatre staff came to collect her. She begged Fernando - begged them all - not to take her away, with outstretched arms and tears in her eyes. Fernando felt helpless and wretched; he held her hands and, unreasonably, told her to relax, it would all be over soon.

Never had he felt so impotent; it was like sending an innocent child to the gallows. As soon as they had taken her, he sat on the edge of her bed and, not for the last time, put his head in his hands and wept.

However, when she came round from the anaesthetic, after surgery, she was a different person; all the depression was gone, she was happy to be alive and looking forward to getting on with life. Fernando was relieved, but knew that her elation would be temporary, for, as the cancer had already spread to the lymph nodes in her armpit; further treatment would be necessary.

Amanda's sutures looked crude and ugly, the wound ran from her left armpit and diagonally down in a straight line to the centre of her chest, where a thin pipe emerged, it was a drain from the lymph glands. It really was a quite shocking sight to behold, not only had the entire breast gone, including the nipple, but also a great deal of surrounding surface flesh. So much so, that her right breast was being pulled, awkwardly, to the middle of her chest.

Fernando assumed that the skin would relax, once the stitches were removed and physiotherapy had begun.

In order for Amanda to be released from the hospital, staff had to be sure that the draining of lymphatic fluid was complete; it took twelve days. During that time, she seemed to be in the bloom of health. It was wonderful for her family to see her so changed and full of energy. However, Fernando was struggling to keep up with the demands of the round trip, from La Joya to the hospital and back, keeping life at home calm for the boys *and* running his business.

When she finally returned home, there was a flurry of visitors and well-wishers, but most of them were embarrassed, or felt a little awkward. Although *she* did not seem to be too bothered by having only one breast, other people were tense. In addition, the very word 'cancer' strikes fear into the hearts of most folks. Within ten days or so, people stopped coming and the telephone ceased ringing, no more cards arrived in the mail and they were back to themselves.

Amanda's oncologist suggested a regime of nine sessions of chemotherapy, at three-week intervals and intensive radiotherapy three times per week for five weeks. She and Fernando agreed and the first chemotherapy took place two days later.

A nurse came into the small room carrying a tray on which were three syringes. Two were very large, perhaps three hundred millilitres and full of clear fluid. The other was about a third of the size, with bright yellow contents.

The doctor prepared Amanda's right arm and inserted a cannula into which the syringes would be fitted. She was very frightened and distressed; Fernando held her left hand as the first syringe-full was pushed slowly into her blood stream.

'Ugh! What's that smell?' Amanda cried, screwing up her face and cringing.

'What smell?' Fernando questioned.

6

'It's like a cross between dry-cleaning fluid and washing-up liquid.' She said, blinking her eyes and shaking her head.

'That's the chemotherapy,' the doctor answered, 'it's circulating around your body and you can smell it from the inside, so to speak.'

'How long will it take to go round?' Amanda asked.

'It's already gone round several times.' Said the doctor, as he emptied the first syringe and attached the second.

'I, I think I'm going to faint…' Amanda said, weakly.

'NURSE!' Shouted the doctor.

Amanda's eyes rolled and she began to slump backwards.

The nurse rushed in, and between them, they managed to get Amanda into a forward position. She was only semi-conscious and started to hyperventilate, immediately the nurse put a paper bag over Amanda's nose and mouth.

Slowly, she calmed and began to regain consciousness. As swiftly as he could, the doctor drained the second syringe, and prepared the smaller third one.

All the while, the nurse and Fernando talked calmly to Amanda, reassuring her and keeping her mind off what was happening, but the chemicals were already having an effect and she became tranquil and dopey.

It took a week for her to recover from that first bout, the sickness was the worst side effect, but on later treatments that was managed with anti-emetics.

The following seven months were an endless round of therapy and recovery; at least Amanda did not lose all of her hair, but she had been weakened extremely by the whole experience.

Fernando was the necessary rock who managed the family and carried the burden with fortitude, but to the detriment of his own well-being; although he kept it hidden, he neglected himself.

Amanda never went back to her job at the gallery. She did not recover enough strength and in 1995 developed severe pain in her left shoulder. All the treatment and trauma of the previous year had been to no avail; she had metastatic bone cancer and a terminal diagnosis.

7

As the cancer spread and no more treatment was available, she needed higher and higher doses of morphine to control the terrible pain that wracked her body.

Eventually, bed-bound and with a syringe driver delivering the analgesia, she drifted in and out of consciousness, but Fernando persisted with his relentless loving care.

In some ways, it was a relief when Amanda died, no more pain for her, but a massive gaping void where she had been in the hearts of those who loved her.

Miguel and Pablo came to terms with the death of their mother as they forged ahead with their careers. For Fernando, there was nothing but to engross himself in work.

Eventually, Miguel left home and Pablo followed soon after. They all knew that the house was too big for Fernando and it forced him to re-evaluate his life as a widower. It was early in 1997 when he relocated to an office in Santa Maria and moved into his penthouse apartment, to start a new life on his own.

*

Shifting slightly in his chair, Fernando used his tiny "piccolo" binoculars to look at the bird-life in the gardens nearby. He also had a better view of the town below and the only high-rise hotel, La Posada, on the edge of the rocky seashore.

Very few people were about; some would open their shops despite it being a recognised holiday, others were perhaps emerging for an early morning promenade but he could see one fellow, out for a jog, wearing a blue and white striped T-shirt. 'Look at him, he has to be a tourist,' he thought, 'you'd never see a local man jogging!' He watched as the man slowly negotiated his way through the winding side streets, past the church and central square and down towards the marina, as he had done, on and off, for a couple of weeks now.

Most of the fishing boats were within the harbour, tied up to the main jetty on the left looking out to sea, their catches being unloaded in large white plastic boxes and packed into waiting vans. It was soon over and the vehicles drove off to deliver their cargo to the local markets, hotels and restaurants. The fishermen dispersed back to their homes, leaving the marina quiet but for the gentle tinkling chimes of yacht mast ropes.

The jogger approached the harbour and, turning right, disappeared behind the old Customs and Revenue House and out of sight. Fernando assumed that he would make his way to the fuel station on the far side of the marina and continue running along the beach but that too was out of his line of view. He watched a final lone fishing boat slowly making its way to the harbour from the north. Although the vessel was very similar to all the other fishing boats there was something odd about this one, but Fernando could not quite determine what it was.

A pale yellow Ford Transit van reversed down to the quay and stopped at the far end where the boat was mooring and two men got out. The vehicle was a low-top, completely plain with no side windows and, like many commercial trucks in Santa Maria, an old model.

Meanwhile, two fishermen unloaded the catch whilst the two on the jetty packed the boxes into the back of the van. There was nothing remarkable about the procedure but for the moment when all four men turned to look towards the Customs and Revenue House. It was only for an instant and they were back at work packing the van.

Fernando downed the last of his coffee, careful to leave the silt at the bottom of his mug.

Employing his binoculars once more, he watched as two more men made their way from the cover of the buildings towards the van. By now, the fishermen were on the jetty and all six stood together briefly; one pointed towards the buildings, the other five looked in that direction and then four climbed into the van and drove off. It did not go far, just up the road from the harbour, turned right into Calle García and disappeared behind the back of La Posada hotel. The boat manoeuvred out of the harbour and headed south.

A pair of parakeets flew by, past Fernando's balcony, screeching as they went. He could hear his neighbours next door, as they busied themselves in their kitchen, soon to be enjoying coffee and the view from their balcony - but nursing hangovers, thought Fernando.

Chapter 2 (Fri 2/Jan/98)

Chief Inspector Cristobal Dorantes was a slim man, just 1.62 metres in height, he had barely been tall enough for the *Cuerpo de Policía Nacional,* but his qualifying grades had been outstanding. His experience was vast: from lecturing to undercover work, from organising raids to being part of them. All of his colleagues respected him. Although he had had his opportunities, he never married, putting his career first.

Time had been kind to him; he did not look like a man on the verge of his retirement.

He was investigating an international drug smuggling ring and as he sat at his office desk speaking on the telephone, he ran his fingers through his thick black hair, and then fingered his bristly moustache.

'Yes Commissioner, my office is here in La Joya and yes, Santa Maria is only just around the coast perhaps ten minutes' drive away...

'Of course I am aware of the need for covert surveillance, Señor...

'...I understand that my part is only a small one in this operation but you can count on my discretion and support...

'Thank you Commissioner, I'll keep you informed.'

Replacing the handset on the cradle, he put his hands behind his head and leaned back in his chair just as the phone rang again; it was one of his subordinates.

'Yes Jose...? A body...? Where...? No, that's not a job for the Maritime Section of the *Guardia Civil...* Very well, tell them I'll be with them straight away.'

The body was not yet in the Mortuary and lay on a trolley guarded by two officers of the *Guardia Civil,* in a small room annexed to the hospital. They leaned over the corpse, careful not to touch it, keeping their arms behind their backs.

'Apparently they're sending *'El Alto'* over to take charge, what do you make of that?' asked one.

'El Alto Dorantes? Really? Ah well, it takes the pressure off us!' mused the other.

The duty Doctor greeted Cristobal at the hospital entrance.

'Chief Inspector, thank you for coming over so quickly, we just have to go through the formalities before handing the body over to Pathology for forensic examination.'

'Yes of course. May I see the deceased?'

'Certainly, please come this way,' said the Doctor and led Cristobal off to the annexe.

'So what do we know Doctor?'

'Well, he was fished out of the water in the marina at Santa Maria this morning at about nine o'clock.' The doctor looked at his notes, then at Cristobal, 'It looks like he's been in the water for a day or so, there's still some rigor mortis. Possibly a yachtsman, who's slipped off his boat, or the pontoon, banged his head and drowned, I've seen one or two cases like that.'

'Perhaps,' said Cristobal whose many years of experience led him to keep an open mind, at least until the post-mortem was completed, 'the *Guardia Civil* are making the necessary enquiries of the Harbour Master to get a manifest of all the vessels and sailors in the marina.'

The Doctor led the way into the room and the two *Guardias* turned to face the door. They stood to attention as Cristobal entered. The height difference was noticeable; the *Guardias* each at 1.9 metres tall looked imposing.

'Relax *hombres*,' said Cristobal, 'show me the body.'

They stood aside and drew back the sheet, which covered the corpse.

'*Dios mio!*' exclaimed Cristobal, recoiling in shocked disbelief, 'I need to speak with your Captain, Alvaro García immediately.'

'Of course Chief Inspector, he's in his office in Santa Maria.'

Alvaro García's office was located in the Town hall where all the local council officers and the Mayor worked. An unremarkable man, with a wife and two teenage children, he had probably reached the pinnacle of his career; he was content with his lot and liked his small domain of Santa Maria, where work for the *Guardia Civil* was steady. Nevertheless, he was not lazy, he knew what needed to be done and when. He was a reliable *Guardia* who could communicate well and command respect from his subordinates; he could delegate.

'Cristobal, good to see you, how are you?' He said, shaking hands warmly with his friend and counterpart.

'I'm fine Alvaro, good to see you too, how's the family?'

'Very well, *gracias*. Now, how about this Chris Baker business...?'

'It's terrible Alvaro, I can't believe it! Just as we thought his intelligence work was paying off! I hope that it's just an unhappy accident. Anyway, I'm going to have to break the news to his family... and the Commissioner. Damn it, it's going to put the surveillance and the investigation back at least a month. The poor fellow, when did he last report in?'

'Well, that's the funny thing, he'd left a message saying that he thought that he was on to something and would get back to us when he was sure.'

'Hmm, when was that Alvaro?'

He picked up some papers from his desk, glanced at them, and then passed them to Cristobal, 'half past seven yesterday morning...'

'So he can't have been in the water for much more than twenty four hours, maximum,' mused Cristobal. 'Who found him?'

'Some kids; they'd gone down to feed the fish that live in the marina and apparently they saw a pair of legs protruding from under the pontoon, and shouted for help. The Harbour Master, a Customs officer and two holidaymakers helped to get the body onto the dockside.'

'Have they all been interviewed?'

'Yes, you have the statements and preliminary reports in your hand.'

'Good work Alvaro, let's go through them now,' Cristobal sat down, 'how about some coffee?'

They divided the documents between them, proceeded to read and re-read the statements, then swapped with each other, digesting every word. Forty minutes and two coffees later, they put the papers down and looked at each other. Cristobal tugged at his moustache.

'I think that we can dismiss what the kids had to say,' said Alvaro.

'I agree. What do you make of the holidaymakers, Herr Gunther and his girlfriend?' asked Cristobal.

13

'Just as they seem, young Germans on holiday with eyes only for each other, they were clearly upset by the event and have nothing to offer by way of useful observations.'

'Just so… Hmm, they're here for another few weeks; send one of the local officers to remind them that we may need to speak with them again.'

'I've already done it, Cristobal.'

'Good man. Now, the Harbour Master's statement is quite interesting, he seems to imply that he'd seen Chris Baker before...?'

'Well, let's have a look at what he was wearing; trainers, white shorts and a football club T-shirt, not much to go on there, lots of English tourists wear such clothing...' said Alvaro.

'Yes but most would be sporting English team colours and logos not a blue and white striped Malaga Football Club shirt,' stated Cristobal as he continued to caress his moustache, 'I think we need to speak with the Harbour Master and the Customs officer.'

'I'll put a call through now,' said Alvaro, 'when can we expect to hear about the autopsy?'

'As today is Friday, I should think we'll have the report by Tuesday or Wednesday. I'll go over there later this afternoon to see how it's going.'

*

Later that day, Cristobal was pacing impatiently along the corridor outside the mortuary where the post mortem was taking place. He had already endured the great disappointment expressed by the Commissioner at Chris Baker's death and also the shock and dismay to the Baker family in England. He needed to clear this up and get on with his job.

The door opened and the pathologist beckoned Cristobal over, 'Chief Inspector, come in please.'

They stood by the mortuary slab, the body naked on top. Cristobal ignored the crudely stitched wound from the top of the sternum to the navel, knowing that the pathologist had finished the internal examination there.

'This man drowned… but only after he'd sustained a severe trauma to the back of his head. He has a fractured skull and I have recovered a few small fragments of what appears to be concrete. It looks as if he might have slipped and cracked his head; in my opinion, unconsciousness came quickly but not before he had tried to get up, then fell into the marina, death soon followed. However, I can't explain the slight bruising there,' he pointed with his gloved hand, 'on the lower part of the ribcage; perhaps he ran into something and was winded. I estimate that he'd been in the water for no more than twenty four hours.'

'Damn it! Thank you Doctor, when can I expect your full report?'

'Give me a couple of days, Wednesday at the latest.'

Chapter 3 (Mon 2/Feb/98)

It was not a long walk from Fernando's apartment to his office; nevertheless, he drove there.

His New Year promise to himself to walk more was a distant memory, now a month later and he had forgotten all about the benefits that the exercise could give him. It was not that he did not enjoy the walk down to town; he just simply could not face the long haul back up to the top! Anyway, he always had his heavy briefcase with him, let alone any shopping that he may have bought!

He parked the car in a side street not far from the Jeweller's shop, above which was his suite of offices. On his walk there, he came to the Real Estate Agents shop with its window full of photographs of properties for sale.

Featured on display was a picturesque villa, which caught his eye, not far along Calle Lorca near where he was standing. It certainly was a fine looking property and very convenient for its proximity to his office and he could afford it... he looked up over his shoulder to his existing home, he could see his own balcony... no, it would be too noisy in town and anyway he loved the birds-eye view from his penthouse. Perhaps it would be worth considering if he had a woman in his life, he thought.

With a light heart, Fernando continued on his way. Just ahead of him walked a lady with long black hair; she was wearing blue jeans and a white T-shirt. She walked with an elegant gait, which Fernando found both alluring and attractive.

He was only a few steps behind her when suddenly an empty green lemonade drink tin clattered to the pavement as a cat jumped down from the wall beside her, ran in front and across the road. The woman was startled and stumbled on the kerb, a Transit van was racing up the road from the harbour directly towards her, and she was going to fall in front of it...! Instinctively, Fernando dropped his briefcase, leapt forward, grabbed the woman and swept her up into his arms, whilst the primrose Transit swerved, then turned right up Calle García. He released her slowly from his grip, his hands sliding down her arms until her hands rested in his.

'Are you all right?' he asked.

16

'Yes, I, I think so...' she said shaking the hair from her eyes, '...*gracias* Señor.'

When she looked up at him, he could see that she was in her mid-forties, medium height, comely and with beautiful hazel eyes.

Fernando was captivated, 'you're welcome,' he said quietly, 'are you sure you're okay?'

'Quite sure,' she responded blushing slightly but still looking directly into his dark eyes. Reluctantly he let go of her hands. She turned, peered up and down the road and crossed. At the opposite pavement, she looked over her shoulder to face Fernando and mouthed, '*Gracias*'. He had watched her all the way across and it was only when he came to say, 'You're welcome' back to her that he realised that his mouth had been agape. She smiled at him, turned and walked away. He followed her with his eyes until she rounded the next corner and disappeared out of sight. After adjusting his necktie, he picked up his briefcase and walked to his office.

'Are you okay?' asked Simon, as Fernando entered the reception area, 'you look a little dazed. Is that blood on your shirtsleeve?'

'What...? Er, no, I don't think so...' he checked the red smudge, 'ah, no, it looks like lipstick.'

Simon walked quizzically over to look, 'What's going on, what's happened?'

Fernando proceeded to tell his assistant of the events that had unfolded on his way to work. However, Simon was right; Fernando *was* dazed and somewhat shocked at what had befallen him. After all, it was not the sort of thing that happened to him normally, or ever, for that matter!

'I think I could do with a coffee please Simon. Remind me, what's on the agenda for today?'

'Coffee's on its way Boss, your first meeting is at noon, the one that was postponed from last week, with... Er...' Simon looked at the diary, '...Cristobal Dorantes, for his bi-annual review.'

Simon showed Cristobal into Fernando's office.

'Cristobal, punctual as ever, just a week late!' Fernando teased, with a smile, and the old friends shook hands warmly, 'please sit down.'

17

'*Gracias*. Yes, sorry about that, I had to go to England.'

'Oh dear, I'm sure that can't have been much of a holiday, not at this time of year; work I suppose?'

'Indeed, I had to repatriate that fellow who was pulled out of the marina last month.'

'A senior officer like you? Sounds intriguing, you'll have to tell me about it later. Now, let's have a look at your investments and pension forecast...'

Cristobal's salary had always been in excess of his needs as a bachelor and with Fernando's help, his investments were growing and paying dividends. He owned his house plus two small apartments, which he rented out to holidaymakers and, having served nearly forty years with the *Policía Nacional*, was looking forward to a healthy pension and retirement.

Forty minutes later and Fernando was able to conclude; 'So in short, that's an overall growth of 9.8% across all of your investments; bonds, savings, stocks and so on. Happy?' he asked.

'With your work, yes of course, I couldn't do it without you.'

'Good, I'm happy too. Now, what's all this about England?'

Cristobal rubbed his fingers across his mouth and moustache and looked Fernando straight in the eye.

'All right Fernando, I know that I can trust you as I would my Doctor or Priest and sometimes these things are worth sharing as it can help to clarify the thoughts...'

Fernando pressed the intercom, 'Simon, it's nearly one o'clock, you can go for lunch now.'

'Thank you, see you later,' was the reply.

'Now, tell me your tale Cristobal.'

'You must have heard about the body which was pulled out of the marina...?'

'Yes, of course.'

'Well, we deliberately held some information back. He was an English Intelligence officer working here as an adviser and observer, I won't go into all the details; anyway he died on New Year's Day. That's why I had to go to England.'

'Oh, I see.'

18

'His name was Chris Baker, he only had aged parents and they were devastated that their only off-spring was dead. Of course, I also had to deal with his superiors who seemed to want to hold me personally responsible for his death.

'I tell you Fernando, I can see why so many tourists who come here on holiday, from the North, are so unruly! It seems to me that they have to contend with appalling weather and a very low standard of living. The public transport is terrible, everyone is in a hurry, they're impolite with anyone who speaks with a foreign accent and their officials are full of double-talk with double standards, I'm glad to be home!'

All the while, Fernando had been studying Cristobal intently, 'New Year's Day, you say? What was this fellow wearing?'

'Huh? Running gear, why?'

'Blue and white striped tee shirt, by any chance?'

'Yes, but we didn't release that information, have you heard some gossip from the harbour or something?'

Fernando walked to the window and beckoned Cristobal over, pointing up he said, 'as you know, my apartment is right at the top, there, I think I saw your man on that morning...'

'What? You must have known that a body had been found why didn't you tell the local *Guardia*?'

'Because it's only now, from what you've told me, that I can see a connection. I had assumed, like everyone else that it was just someone who'd drowned after too much celebrating on New Year's Eve! You said that you'd kept some information back regarding the matter. Now I come to think of it, there were others in the marina at the time...'

Cristobal interrupted, 'how good was your view of them, from up there?'

'Let's go up and you can see, I'll tell you what I remember as I'm sure to have more information in which you will be interested. I'll just check my appointments...' He walked through to reception and checked the diary, '...Er, no, nothing until four o'clock. If we're going now, I'd better leave Simon a note.'

'Why not call him on his mobile phone? He's got one, I assume?'

19

'Yes of course, but unlike La Joya where the cellular signal is good, here in Santa Maria because of the tall cliffs and hills the signal is virtually non-existent. Although, they have been working on the radio repeaters on the top of La Posada for over a year now, but who knows when they'll be operational!'

Fernando stuck the hastily written note on the outside of the office door. They walked in silence round to Fernando's car and within a few minutes were up at his apartment.

'Come through, here, onto the balcony.' Fernando insisted and gave Cristobal a few moments to familiarise himself with the view.

'I'd forgotten what a fabulous *mirador* you have! And you still live here alone. You need to find another woman to share it with!'

'Well, you're a bachelor, you cope all right! Actually, I had hoped that one day a rich widow would come in for financial advice as I don't get out much and I'm certainly not interested in singles' bars! Perhaps I should join a fitness club, or something?' he said, patting his midriff.

'Perhaps you should, or dance classes; it takes two to tango, you know!' Cristobal said with a grin.

Early afternoon sun was lighting the town from the south west, somewhat in their eyes, as it was quite low in the sky and early in the year.

They could see the cars and people in the streets below, small and large pleasure boats coming and going from the harbour, the sounds of every-day life drifting up and blending with birdsongs from the gardens nearby.

Cristobal studied the scene intently. He could see on the horizon, cloud-capped La Goma and in the near distance, both water and jet skiers. The Vista to the north of majestic cliffs running away into the far distance and falling sheer into the ocean, with waves breaking white at their feet. Nearby, the technicians on the top of La Posada, presumably working on the telecommunications systems. He looked at Fernando.

'Tell me what you saw amigo.'

'Please sit down,' Fernando indicated to his own preferred seat, 'that's where I usually sit to enjoy the view.'

He then proceeded to recall the events of New Year's Day. He spoke of the lambency, which grew into early daylight, of the fishing boats mobbed by

20

their attendant gulls, the unloading at the harbour of the vessels' catches. He pointed out the route that Chris Baker's fateful run had taken and where Fernando had lost sight of him, of the odd lone boat, the pale yellow van and the two other men who appeared from the Customs buildings.

Cristobal had been following Fernando's directions of Baker's route and, understanding the perspective of the land and seascape; he turned and looked at Fernando.

'What was it about the boat that was unremarkable and yet memorable? Was it bigger, smaller, a different colour perhaps? Have you seen it since?'

'No, I haven't noticed it since but I haven't been looking for it and I can't put my finger on what was different about it; it looked just like all the other fishing boats...' Fernando hesitated, '...but I think I may have seen the van... today, this morning, at about ten o'clock... a cat knocked a discarded green lemonade drink tin off a wall, the clatter and suddenness of it startled a woman walking just in front of me and she nearly fell in front of the van which then turned up Calle García.'

Fernando looked at Cristobal who was leaning forward in his chair, elbows on the table, his chin cupped in his hands.

Looking up, Cristobal said, 'I don't suppose you got the registration number? No, of course not. So, what's up Calle García? There's the small carpark at the back of La Posada, access to their gardens and the old Citizens' Social Services Offices... hmm, I wonder...' he mused. 'Fernando, I'd like to get my colleague Captain Alvaro García of the local *Guardia Civil* up here, would that be acceptable?'

'Yes, of course.'

Cristobal removed his mobile phone from its holster on his belt and pulled up the antenna.

'Hmm, I see what you mean about the weak signal,' he said looking at the small screen, 'I'll try it anyway; there might be enough strength up here...' Scrolling through the contacts list, he soon found Alvaro's office number.

'Alvaro it's Cristobal. Are you free for half an hour and can you get a car to bring you to the top carpark up Calle Los Pinos? That's great, I'll meet you in five minutes, and oh, please can you bring Chris Baker's diary and your binoculars with you? Thanks.'

21

Cristobal was waiting when Alvaro arrived, and introduced him to Fernando who went to make coffee.

The two officers stood to one side of the balcony and quietly discussed Fernando. Cristobal assured Alvaro of Fernando's probity and explained how they first met at the *Escuela Nacional de Policía* and been close friends ever since and that he could be a great asset to them now. Soon all three men were standing together looking at the town below.

Having brought Alvaro up to date, Cristobal said, 'Now, Fernando, we know that cocaine is being smuggled from South America to Europe via our archipelago and we're fairly certain that Santa Maria is a staging post. The problem is that well-organised, well-funded professional criminals are running the operation. The Europol Drugs Unit, EDU, is in charge of the overall investigation which is why we had help from Chris Baker; we're just a few provincial Lawmen with limited resources, and need all the help we can get.'

'I understand. So you think that Baker's death may be the link in the chain of events that could open up your part of the investigation?' Fernando responded.

'Correct,' said Alvaro. 'We know that he was on to something and from what you've said we think it could be to do with this boat or van.'

Cristobal picked up the binoculars and examined the vessels in the marina, then scanned up and down the coast finally settling on La Posada and Calle García. 'Hmm, I can't resolve the fishing boat numbers nor car registrations from here with these,' he said looking at the specification of the binoculars.

'Hold on, I have an idea...' said Fernando, 'give me a minute...'

Leaving Cristobal and Alvaro in deep discussion, Fernando briskly made his way to a little used storage room in an annexe to his apartment, returning several minutes later. He was hugging what looked like the cumbersome rag-wrapped corpse of an Egyptian Mummy.

'*Diablo!*' exclaimed Cristobal, 'what is that?'

Fernando carefully held on to the item with one hand and unwound the cloths with his other to reveal a tripod baring a compact but large aperture reflector telescope. 'I'd forgotten all about this; I bought it for my son

22

Miguel, he was a keen astronomer as a teenager. Now, let's see if I can get it set up.'

Adjusting the legs so that the instrument was comfortable to use whilst seated, he carefully trained the telescope on the marina. Setting for maximum field of view, he swapped the eyepiece to increase the magnification and brought the picture into focus. 'There *caballeros*, care to take a look?'

Alvaro was keen to see, *'Guau!* Look at that! No problem reading registration numbers now! Try it Cristobal.'

The men swapped places. Cristobal gently traversed his vision in the eyepiece across from the marina to La Posada, along Calle García and back down the road to the harbour. He looked up at Alvaro, and then to Fernando, 'I think that I have a little job for you,' he said with a wry smile.

'You want me to keep a look out for the boat and van, don't you?' queried Fernando.

'Yes please. I'd suggest one of our men but I think that it would be an imposition, we can't spare anyone and *you* know what you're looking for.'

'But that would be like trying to find a black cat at midnight,' Fernando protested, 'what do I have to go on?'

'Hmm, well let's see,' said Alvaro, 'you saw the van today, the 2nd of February at about ten o'clock, right? And, by your account you saw both van and boat on New Year's Day, Thursday 1st of January at about nine o'clock, so let's look at Baker's diary...' Fernando leaned over the table to look as Alvaro leafed back through to January. 'There, a hash symbol on Thursday 1st, and a number 9... December 12th, Friday, hash and a number ten and November... look, on Tuesday 11th the same hash and a number nine...'

'There is a pattern there,' said Cristobal, who had been scribbling on his notepad, 'each day number is the same as the month and the alternating nine and ten correspond with our known times that the van has been seen by Fernando. I suspect that the next appearance will be on...' He reached for Alvaro to pass Baker's diary, '...on Tuesday the 3rd of March at nine o'clock in the morning. To be sure, Fernando, I'd like you to check each morning from, say, eight o'clock. I don't think that you'll see anything at all until the 3rd of March, though. If we're right, at least Chris Baker's time here wasn't wasted.'

23

'That's no problem,' said Fernando, 'I'll get the necessary registration numbers and anything else that I think maybe of importance. Do you want me to report directly to you, Cristobal?'

'Er, no, as I'm in La Joya most of the time you'd better liaise with Alvaro. It might be an idea to print up some sort of spreadsheet to fill in. *Gracias* Fernando,' he said, reaching out to shake the hand of his friend, 'you've been a great help, I'm only sorry that this will not be a job that we can pay you for! Right, we'd better let you get back to your office. Alvaro I'll go with you, we have much to discuss. I'll pick up my car later.'

Chapter 4 (Tues 3/Mar/98)

The daily ritual of watching the fishing boats arriving at the harbour was losing none of its appeal for Fernando. Alvaro had supplied carbon paper and printed reams of an ambitious spreadsheet with all of the relevant boxes for Fernando to fill in. It included date, vessel number, name and colour, time of arrival, from which direction each boat approached the harbour, what make and colour of van attended each boat, number of persons on each boat and van, time of departure, direction taken away from the harbour, weather conditions, observations, etc.

However, he was slightly disappointed when Tuesday 3rd March came without any sightings of the boat or van. He telephoned Alvaro who was noncommittal but said that he would speak with Cristobal and call back later. 'Perhaps Cristobal was wrong about the pattern,' thought Fernando as he prepared himself for work.

Having parked his car, briefcase in hand, Fernando proceeded to his office giving only a passing glance to the Real Estate Agent's window but he slowed his pace and paused as he approached the corner of Calle Lorca. There was a red Cola tin on the wall, just as there had been a green lemonade tin on the 2nd February, he was sure that he hadn't seen such a thing since, on his walk to work...

*

Later that morning Simon buzzed through on the intercom to inform Fernando that Cristobal was on the phone; the men exchanged greetings then got straight down to business.

'So, a no-show this morning?' asked Cristobal.

'That's right, do you think that we might have misread Baker's diary?'

'No, I'm more convinced now that we're on the right track.' Cristobal responded cryptically.

'Oh, how so?' quizzed Fernando.

'I cannot say right now, sorry. Please keep observing *amigo*. I tell you what; can Alvaro and I meet you at your apartment this Saturday morning, that's the seventh at eleven o'clock?'

25

'Er, yes that's fine, see you then.'

*

(Sat 7/3/98)

The three men gathered on Fernando's balcony, it was a fine day and the view as attractive as ever. Bougainvillea that had been quite dull over the wintertime was now in full bloom with magenta and white tumbling over from Fernando's rooftop and flooding across the terrace.

He had pushed the telescope and a chair into the overgrowth so that he could view the harbour secretly. Clandestine surveillance was new to him and he did not want to jeopardise the investigation by compromising his position in case someone on a boat had just such a visual aid and may see him!

They sat around the small table and scrutinised the spreadsheet diary. There was nothing unusual; all the boats coming and going were as expected plus a few odd visitors. Together they collated them with the manifests from the Harbour Master on Alvaro's nominally portable laptop computer. They ignored all of the Santa Maria fishing boats and those given over to tourism. The vessels registered abroad, including ocean going yachts, had their names and numbers listed by Alvaro. Also of special interest was the Harbour Master's list of fishing boats, which had visited in the past six months but registered elsewhere in the archipelago.

'Right,' said Cristobal, directly to Fernando, 'Alvaro is already aware of what I'm about to tell you.'

Fernando looked from Cristobal to Alvaro and back again.

'This whole operation,' Cristobal continued, 'is being overseen as you know, by the EDU, and in an attempt to disrupt the supply of cocaine into Europe, an manoeuvre was conducted by their Special Services in the ocean about 2500 kilometres south west from here.'

He could see that Fernando was struggling to comprehend. Alvaro took over, 'We already know that the drugs are being shipped to Europe from South America, primarily via Venezuela from Colombia, right?'

Fernando nodded affirmative and Alvaro resumed.

26

'Well, the smugglers use what look like genuine commercial ships, with genuine cargo but crewed almost entirely by mercenaries in the pay of the drug barons. They load up with beverages, spirits, vinegar, cocoa, anything that can be exported legitimately, plus the cocaine. They make monthly trips to the Netherlands and Belgium and other places but they unload their contraband to smaller vessels at various mid Atlantic rendezvous' west of here.'

Cristobal came back in, 'So the EDU launched a covert military action to intercept one such cargo vessel before it could make its rendezvous...' He looked directly at Fernando, 'It was at the end of last month - middle of the night - when half a dozen Special Services boats approached the smugglers, the servicemen got on-board without a shot being fired, held them, located and confiscated the cocaine, weapons, et cetera and left them to it...'

'What...? You mean they just left the smugglers alone, no arrests, nothing? Just let them carry on to Amsterdam, or wherever?' Fernando asked incredulously.

'Well actually, they waited twenty four hours, then went to Amsterdam to drop the legal cargo then straight back to Port of Guairá, Caracas,' interjected Alvaro, 'the Servicemen planted their own GPS – Global Positioning System – tracking device on the ship!'

'Hah!' Declared Fernando, 'So they never made the meeting with any other vessels and that's why I didn't see any activity four days ago! Also, there was a red Cola tin on the wall, by Calle García where that green tin was before...perhaps there's a link? What do you think happened when they got back to Venezuela? And why did they wait for a whole day before returning?'

'Who knows?' Shrugged Cristobal, 'Perhaps they needed time to sort out what to tell their bosses? At least unloading the cargo in Europe would not only be legitimate but also cover some of the loss...' He leaned across the table and held Fernando's gaze, 'Fernando, we're dealing with very, *very* unsavoury characters here, powerful people who'll cheat and blackmail, coerce, assault, injure even murder anyone who gets in their way. They have no respect for law and order only for the cartel or overlord and, of course, money. Perhaps their superiors just put it down to experience, maybe the vessel has been renamed and a new crew on-board? One thing is for sure; the operation will continue after they lie low for a while. They have too much at stake and a lucrative market in Europe. A few sailors who lose their cargo are probably dispensable...'

Fernando's face paled as he began to comprehend that those sailors may have been tortured or killed, and who knows about any further repercussions to any of their families? It became clear to him that he was now embroiled in a dark web of underworld illegality and his life would probably never be the same again. Who could say what would happen next? What started out as an exciting little adventure, helping his old friend, had suddenly taken a very serious and sinister turn. He would still have to continue as normal but now he would also be playing a pivotal role in a parallel life to that of being a financial adviser, an antithesis. All of this sped through his mind. Was he up to it? Could he do it – did he *want* to do it? There would be no glory, he would play an invisible part – at least he probably would not face any danger – would he? His reverie was broken by Cristobal.

'Don't dwell on it my friend, our job is simply to piece together what happens on our patch, we're only one small link in the chain.' Cristobal's many years in law enforcement had given him great perception and his ability to read Fernando's face helped to bring perspective.

'So what's our next move?' requested Fernando, including himself, now fully committed to his new double life.

Alvaro responded, 'Cristobal and I will continue to collate all this information,' he gesticulated to the paperwork and laptop on the table before them, 'and our current lines of enquiry. We'd like you to carry on doing exactly as you have been, let's see what happens at 10a.m. on the fourth of April.'

Reaching inside his jacket Alvaro produced a hand-held, two-way, walkie-talkie radio and from another pocket a telescopic antenna which he screwed into the top. Switching the set on, he extended the aerial to its fullest, about a metre, he passed it to Fernando and proceeded to talk him through its functions. 'Here, I've got a copy of the instructions for you as well. Probably best not to tell anyone that you have this, Fernando, as its *Guardia* property! And only use it in an utmost emergency!'

'I understand. Er… Roger, I should say,' Fernando responded with a wry smile.

Cristobal put his hand on Fernando's shoulder, looked him in the eye and said, '*Gracias amigo*, you're a good man, and I'm sure that your police training will serve you well.' Then he and Alvaro took then their leave.

Fernando sat back down at the table and his glance shifted from the carbon-copy spreadsheets, to his telescope, then to the harbour and to the walkie-talkie. He stood up and realised he was both excited and somewhat frightened at the same time, perhaps they were the same thing? No, he was not out of his depth. He was perfectly capable of performing this simple act of covert espionage! Moreover, Cristobal was right; Fernando's years in Police school should help. Until the meeting, he had only considered himself an adjunct supplying the authorities with a bit of extra information, but he now realised that the accuracy of his fact-finding might be crucial to the investigation.

Taking a deep breath, he decided to apply himself to this task with the same responsibility as if he were investing someone's hard-earned cash.

Casting his mind back to the beginning of the year he watched, in his mind's eye, the events which led to the small fishing boat unloading at the harbour. He tried to playback the sequence in reverse, repeatedly; he saw that the boat approached from the north, it was alone… there were no gulls following, or certainly very few, if any!

'No gulls!' he cried aloud, 'So *that* was what was so different! *Diablo*, A fishing boat with no fish and even the birds knew!'

However, there was no need to rush this information to Cristobal as the link had already been made with this vessel, but it cleared things in Fernando's mind.

He studied the coastline to the north, with his telescope, from the harbour past the small beach of Playa Piqueña, beyond Punta Piqueña, the Playa de los Chicos hidden from view and on up to Punta Del Acantilados with the final tip of Punta Del Tiempo just visible in the far distant haze. He scanned back again pausing at Punta Piqueña and letting his mind wonder and he could see, the mountains above Playa de los Chicos… 'Playa de los Chicos…? I wonder…' he thought.

He could see his wife and their two young sons walking ahead of him down the winding track to Señor Arrabal's finca. In his mind's eye, he could see the old man waving from his porch. The stream from Fuente Armarga was dancing down the ravine on their right as they descended towards the tiny beach. Amanda and the boys were singing as they all stopped at the mirador; a flattish rocky area, from which he pointed out various landmarks to his young family...

A sudden screech from a parakeet in a nearby garden shook Fernando from his reminiscence. He looked out to the town and harbour below, at people going about their daily business, the normal bustle of a Saturday afternoon, holidaymakers and visitors enjoying the glorious weather and natural beauty of Santa Maria. Only when a tear ran down his cheek did he feel the intense melancholy of his solitary life. He stood up, pulled his shoulders back and said aloud, 'Right, come on Fernando, you're made of stern stuff! What would Amanda say? *"There's a job to be done and it won't get finished unless you start it!"* Now where are my walking boots?'

He needed to look at Playa de los Chicos again.

Chapter 5 (Sat 7/3/98)

Fernando spent the rest of Saturday afternoon locating his old hiking gear; it had been many years since he had last worn his walking boots, lightweight thorn resistant trousers and jacket. The Goretex boots still had plenty of life left in them and although the trousers were tugged and faded here and there, they were perfectly serviceable. His jacket was really for high altitude walking and perfectly suited for climbing the snow-capped *Montaña de la Caldera,* not low altitude hill walking, so he selected his windproof breathable fleece. Walking pole, gloves, cap and a small backpack for his water bottle, binoculars and his new Nikon digital camera, he would be ready to go first thing next morning.

(Sun 8/3/98)

A thin silvery hue covered the sky as Fernando drove out of Santa Maria, up the winding hairpin bends to *Fuente Armarga Del Cerro,* where the temperature would be a few degrees lower than at the coast.

Thick cloud was clinging to the sides of Montaña de la Caldera, if they descended to lower altitudes then it could mean rain, particularly to the north but it would be unusual here, he thought.

He had not driven that way for a long while; all his trips out of Santa Maria took him to bigger towns or even to the capital. He had forgotten how beautiful this side of the island was; the more he had climbed the better the view of the coast to his left. Ahead and on his right; the haphazard slopes of volcanic rock boulders tamed by the smooth asphalt road, clumps of dried grasses being wafted by the wind, occasional prickly pear cactus, and agaves with their spear-spikes like fingers pointing skywards, coming into their once-in-a-lifetime flowering. After about thirty minutes' driving time the road levelled out, then began descending to the village valley.

Eventually he arrived to the view that he was expecting; the village of Fuente Armarga Del Cerro - Bitter Spring of the Hills - so called due to the taste of the spring water which emanated at the top of the valley. Melting snow from the distant Montaña de la Caldera and rainwater, which had percolated through the volcanic rocks from the hills above the village, picked up various minerals on its way through. Nevertheless, it helped to irrigate an otherwise barren valley into a veritable verdant paradise.

Tiny white houses, like sugar cubes, tumbled down the hillsides, and settled at the bottom. Many of the houses and *fincas* higher up the valley were in ruins, due to abandonment when the children of farmers decided to leave for a better life in the wealthy towns on the coast. However, a couple of small bars, restaurants and shops managed to stay solvent thanks to the richness of produce that the land provided.

Fernando rolled his car gently to a halt outside *El Papagayo*. 'I wonder if Paco Martín still runs this bar?' he thought, as he took his boots and fleece from the back seat and prepared himself for his trek.

It was midmorning and the door to the bar was open. He entered and there was Paco mopping the tiled floor. Chairs were stacked on the tables and all the windows were open. A teenage girl busied herself loading the chilled glass displays at the bar with various *tapas* and a young male was cleaning the *plancha*. Flamenco music was playing in the background but echoing around the bar as if it were a cavern.

Now aged in his late-thirties, Paco had taken over from his father in the 1980's, Fernando assumed both of the youngsters working in the bar to be Paco's offspring. He was a tall, rotund fellow with cropped short black hair, and a jovial grin permanently etched onto his face. Over his white shirt and black trousers, he was wearing a stained chef's apron.

'Good day, Paco,' called Fernando upon entering the room.

Paco looked up and hesitated briefly, 'Señor Fernández?' he asked.

'That's right, how are you?' Fernando enquired, whilst shaking the hand of the bar-owner.

'I'm as busy as I want to be!' he responded as he leaned on his mop, 'you haven't been here for a while, how are you? I see you've lost a little hair and shaved off your moustache!' he teased.

Fernando smiled, responding, 'And you've put on a little weight!' he joked, 'yes, I've been busy too. You know I lost my wife?'

'Yes I heard, I'm very sorry, how are your boys, they must be men now?'

'Both graduated and working abroad. Are these your kids?' Fernando asked, nodding to the two working behind the bar.

'Indeed they are,' Paco said proudly, 'Juan and Julia, this trade is in their blood!'

Paco made them a coffee each, took a couple of chairs down and as they sat proceeded to discuss what had happened to each of them over the last few years. An easy twenty minutes in conversation slipped by before Fernando remembered why he was there.

'So I'm off for a walk down to Playa de los Chicos, if I can remember the way.'

'All right but it is quite a distance remember, probably further than you recall and quite a hard slog back up. No one goes that way these days and, remember the stream? It's been quite wet uphill from here and the snows on the mountain are starting to thaw. Brought any food with you? No, I guessed not,' Paco looked over his shoulder and called to Julia to make a ham and cheese *bocadillo*, 'you're bound to need some sustenance, call back in when you return and we'll have a *cerveza* together.'

Fernando proffered some money for the coffee and bocadillo, which Paco refused, Fernando said, 'that's very kind of you, and yes I will call in and see you later.'

Giving no thought to the lowering sky and with his walking pole in hand, Fernando strode off to the path to Playa de los Chicos. The going was very easy whilst in the confines of the village; plenty of people took advantage of the magnificent view of the stream and across the valley. The outlook was not lost on Fernando; the craggy rough boulders of the hillsides were a marvel of volcanic hues interspersed with colonising vegetation, here and there even a pine tree was beginning to get a foothold. It had been hundreds of years since Montaña de la Caldera last threw out lava or ash of any kind.

Nearer to the watercourse the greener it became, many less hardy plants surviving, even a few alpine-like flowers. With the splashing water to the right and a good wide path ahead, Fernando made excellent progress quickly leaving the last of the buildings behind.

There was much more of a ravine further on where numerous springs added to the watershed, which crashed and tumbled on its way down to the sea. The track descended steadily and Fernando remembered that it was wide enough for Señor Arrabal's donkey and cart. The gorge disappeared from view as the trail rounded a bluff but the constant sound of the gushing water echoed between the walls of the ravine. He did not notice that the way was unkempt, overgrown at the sides and showed no signs nor tracks of a cart, donkey or human footprints.

Señor Arrabal's *finca rustica* was a sad sight for Fernando to observe; he recalled a well-kept and tidy area in front of the building, with open sheds for a donkey and a few goats. There used to be a shaded porch attached to the whitewashed stone walls of the *finca*. It once had a green painted door, small windows and shutters, and over-topped with a terracotta pan-tiled roof. Now all was derelict and decrepit, no signs of human activity, just an old abandoned dwelling, home only to wildlife.

With his walking pole, he pushed on the half-open door and peered inside. Light flooded in to the room but was mainly from the gaping hole in the roof; it lit the tiled floor, now littered with the mud and reeds, which had once held the pan-tiles. There were a few sticks of termite-ridden furniture and, hanging on the wall, an old faded picture of Señor Arrabal, wearing baggy trousers, jacket and a straw hat, standing with his wife. Fernando felt a pang of despondency at the desolation that he beheld and slowly withdrew.

He looked about; an old and unkempt rose bush was in flower and rambling its way over the ruins, some almond trees were in late blossom and, here and there, he could hear the chirruping of small birds. The sun briefly cut through the grey clouds and lit up a patch of still whitewashed wall, whereupon a gecko darted out to gain a little heat. It served to remind Fernando that life finds a way to continue despite such evident abandonment. Strangely, he felt invigorated not at all downhearted and took out his water bottle for an energising draught.

Locating the next part of the route was not as straightforward as Fernando had thought; apparently, it had not been trodden for a long time. He knew the direction, which was obvious; he only needed the ravine to his right and the old farmland to his left. Intuition led him to the overgrown trail. Although he was very glad that he had brought his walking aid and thorn-proof trousers, as the coarse undergrowth and brambles marred his progress. In places, it was considerably steeper and more treacherous than he recollected and the sound of the water down in the ravine was getting louder.

Eventually, the gulley widened and he could see the water as it gushed down; tumbling over the boulders in the valley but it was slowing and becoming less noisy. However, the path did not get any easier; it was narrowing with a sheer cliff to the left and quite a precipitous drop down to the right. Taking it very gradually, Fernando negotiated his way down, natural steps in the rock helped to keep his progress steady. His view to the coast was completely hidden as the valley curved round to the left and the cliff-face beside him was almost vertical, fortunately the track was widening even though there was a great deal of vegetation to negotiate. Nobody had been down here for a long time, he thought.

The sound of bright water was diminishing and replaced by a steady deep rumble as Fernando rounded a promontory. He had been looking down, to maintain his surefooted progress, now he looked up and was finally greeted with the vista of his memory.

Allowing his eyes to wander from right to left; the valley, although still steep, had broadened and held a small *embalse*, a lake fringed with aquatic plants. Like an infinity swimming pool, the water tumbled over the far end of the small reservoir, and a fine mist drifted up from the cascade to the beach, perhaps fifty metres below.

Hemmed in by the cliffs, the curving beach was lapped by the Atlantic Ocean waves. A thin silver horizon showed that the sun was shining, just not on the land. Away from the towering sea cliff to the left, Fernando could just make out the hazy coastline farther south from Santa Maria.

An untouched stupendous spectacle, he soaked in the view for a few minutes and thought of Amanda.

Looking down to the large, flat ledge on which he was standing, he was horrified to see a discarded newspaper, empty drinks tins and other detritus strewn about. '*Diablo*!' he exclaimed out loud realising that this was not the sacrosanct place he thought it to be. He wheeled round and looked at the track from which he had arrived; it was virtually non-existent. He then looked at the path, which traversed its way down to the beach; it was well trodden!

'Who could defile such a place?' he thought. Then he remembered why he was there, not just to rekindle his memory of the past but to satisfy his hunch that Playa de los Chicos had something to do with the smuggling operation.

Then another rumbling disturbed his thoughts but it was his stomach – he realised that he had not eaten since breakfast and it was now the middle of the afternoon.

Fernando unloaded his backpack and, using one hand began to consume the bocadillo, with the other, he scanned the beach and sea using the binoculars.

He counted several white buoys just within the confines of the bay and more out to sea and assumed them to mark lobster or crab pots. On the beach, he could see a dark object on the sand by where the path started its ascent; it was a discarded outboard motor. Also nearby there were lobster pots, pink buoys and some blue nylon rope.

After completing the snack, he began to take photos' of the scene, and then turned his attention to the rubbish, which was scattered about the ledge.

Reaching for the newspaper, he felt disgust at the insensitivity of the litterers. It was the local paper: *La Hoja Informativa* and Fernando recognised the headline from the previous week, he looked at the date; it was Tuesday the Third of March.

'*Diablo*! So, this *could* be the lookout for the local smugglers!

He was about to put the newspaper in his bag but thought better of it, instead he photographed it and all the other rubbish. Better to leave the place as he found it, just in case.

Having one last look around, he carefully stepped back onto the path and pushed the undergrowth across. Glancing up to the leaden sky and then to his wristwatch; he realised that there would only be a couple of hours' daylight left, 'I'd better get moving!' he thought.

Paco was right; it was a hard slog back uphill but Fernando trudged on oblivious of the undergrowth catching and tugging at his clothes. He just did not want to lose his step and kept his eyes on the rocky path before him, though he stumbled regularly. The thought of reaching the bar and a welcoming beer burned bright in his mind. He trudged on but soon became aware that the noise of the water in the gully below was gaining in volume.

'*Mierda*!' he cried out, with the realisation that a flash flood of snowmelt from the mountain could be heading down the valley. He quickened his pace as best as he could; the light was fading fast, 'If I can just get back to Señor Arrabal's…' he thought, 'at least I'll be within striking distance of Fuente Armarga.'

PART 2

Chapter 6 (Sun 8/3/98)

Stumbling and groping his way along the rocky path, Fernando held his walking pole in his left hand and felt ahead with his right. In the chasm, the crashing sound of the torrent was spurring him onwards and back up to the ruined *finca* of Señor Arrabal. It was virtually dark but his eyes had adjusted and he had just enough night-vision to keep going, although very slowly.

Undergrowth and twisted vegetation grabbed at his trousers and jacket but luckily his gloves were saving his hands from lacerations. He could feel the beads of sweat on his brow forming into more organised globules, running down and dripping off his eyebrows and nose. 'Why did I linger so long?' he thought, as he stubbed his toe once again, dropping him to his knees, '*Gilipollas!*' he shouted at himself. Standing erect and taking a deep breath, he stood still for a moment in order to regain his composure.

The scents of wild oregano mixed with the earthy dampness emanating from the watercourse assailed his nostrils; at least there was something pleasant about this return journey! Wiping the perspiration from his forehead with the back of his hand, he started once again. Toiling on, every step was beginning to drain him of strength, 'I'll stop for a drink of water when I get to the *finca*,' he decided. Finally, the looming silhouette of the ruin rewarded him and he knew that the going would be easier ahead.

Lifting the bag from his back, he found the water bottle and took a big mouthful, 'I'd better save some,' he thought, 'I may need more before I get back to Paco's.' With the bag between his feet, he sat and leaned his back against the old stone wall of the *finca* and looked up. The sky was clearing and he glimpsed a few stars between the tattered clouds, 'if only there was a moon to light my way,' he thought but it was yet to rise and was on the opposite side of the mountain!

Then it came to him; his camera had a display screen! He rummaged in his bag and took out the Nikon but hesitated before sliding open the cover and switching it on. The small screen on the back of the Coolpix 300 would be very bright; perhaps it alone would be sufficient light for his needs? Keeping his hand over the back of the camera and with the lens pointing towards him, he switched it on, and then slowly removed his hand. It was enough to light

40

the ground immediately ahead of his feet, 'it might be sufficient,' he thought and stood up to be sure. Not as bright as he was hoping for, he suddenly remembered that the camera also had a built-in flash! He pressed the button in order to take a picture but forgot to turn the camera around. The flash went off in his face burning its brightness directly onto his retinas. Too shocked to cry out, he dropped the camera and stumbled backwards against the *finca* wall. All of his acquired night-vision was totally gone; all he could see was the permanent blaze of the after-image.

Fernando had no idea how long he sat, waiting for the flare in his eyes to subside. He had tried cupping his hands over his face in a vain attempt to relieve his suffering but to no avail.

Eventually, he floundered and fumbled about on the ground in order to locate the source of his distress. The camera either had gone into standby mode or switched off, whichever it showed no sign of its whereabouts. However, he grovelled around on his hands and knees and was lucky to find it less than a metre away.

He had begun to regain some of his sight and decided to retry the flash idea but this time being sure to hold the camera lens away from him! With the Nikon close to his chest, he pressed the button but nothing happened, perhaps it was damaged? Slowly rotating the camera forward, there was no image on the screen; he checked and found it had gone on to stand-by. Carefully sliding the switch, the camera came to life so he tried again. His vision was not fully recovered but he determined to push on.

Grabbing his bag and pole, he stood with the old building behind him and fired the camera; the flash was intense as it momentarily lit up the area about him. It was brief but enough to see where the track back to Fuente Amarga lay. Using the pole as a blind man would; sweeping it side to side as he went, he determined that he could make about ten steps before having to reshoot the camera. Thus, he proceeded on his way, finally rounding a bend and seeing the glow of lights from the village in the distance.

Breathing a sigh of relief, Fernando stopped for a well-earned swig of the last of his water. When he decided to move on, he could see that the camera flash was not as bright as it had been.

'*Que demonias*, the batteries are dying!' he said aloud in self-admonition.

41

That was when he heard a sound ahead, above the volume of the gushing water in the gulley to his left. He stood motionless, closed his eyes and strained his ears… there it was again, a man's voice… calling… 'What is he calling?' Fernando listened and waited.

'Señor Fernández?'

There it was again, distant but clear, now he was sure!

'*Hola*,' Fernando cried, 'over here, over here! Who's that?'

'Wait there Señor, I'll come to you, I'm Juan Martín, Paco's son.'

Fernando could see the joggling beam of an intense torchlight heading towards him. He stopped and waited, leaning on his walking pole, 'I'd better shield my eyes,' he thought, 'I don't want to be blinded again.'

At length, keeping the lamplight cast down, Juan came up to him and extended his hand. Fernando removed his glove and they shook hands warmly.

'My father sent me to look for you, he noticed that your car was still outside the Bar and as it's getting late, he assumed that you may have got into some difficulties,' Juan stated clearly.

'Well, I'm very pleased to see you Juan and I'm very grateful that your father has sent you out to find me. I think that I undertook too much today!' Fernando responded weakly.

'I saw some flashes, was that you?' Juan enquired.

'Yes, I was using my camera to help light my way.'

'Very good, do you need any help to walk; you do look a little worse for wear, if I may say so.'

It was true; Fernando presented quite a pitiful sight. It was at this point he realised that his clothes were soaked in sweat, which had cooled; he shivered and almost felt a faint coming on but Juan helped him to sit for a moment.

As Fernando had lost his hat, his head and face bore the signs of small scratches. In addition, his gloves had lost some of their dye, which, along with dirt, had rubbed off onto his face. His jacket had several tears, rips and pulls but his trousers were in remarkably good condition though very grubby, particularly at the knees. The Gortex boots were not too bad; they just looked even more old and tatty than earlier that day.

'Here,' Juan said and produced a small chocolate bar from his pocket, 'eat this.'

Fernando consumed the confectionary eagerly. He soon felt the effects of the sugar, soothing his stomach and boosting his energy levels and was on his feet in no time at all, although he felt that he ached all over.

'*Gracias* Juan, I'm ready, *vamos amigo!*'

Juan took the rucksack and they trudged back to El Papagayo.

Quite a lively din was emanating from the bar and as soon as they entered, Paco left his duties and led Fernando to a small table. Juan immediately disappeared into the kitchen whilst his father and Fernando were in conversation. Julia approached and placed two glasses down on to the table

'Here Señor, a Cola for energy and small *Brandy de Jerez* for warmth,' she smiled and went back to her duties.

'Well Paco, I can't thank you enough for this and sending Juan out to find me!'

'You're welcome. Now look, the lavatories are just over there, remember? There is plenty of hot water and a mirror. Please freshen up.'

Fernando took his leave of Paco and was quite shocked at how rough he looked, but a good wash made him feel much better.

'*Gracias* Paco, I still look a bit of a mess, I know. Sorry to have put you to so much trouble,' he said, as he sat back down at the table.

'Please stop thanking me *amigo*; it is I who should be thanking you!'

'What do you mean...?' Fernando began to ask but was interrupted by Juan who, in one hand held a napkin, cutlery and a chunk of bread, in the other he bore a large bowl of warm *callos,* 'This should restore you Señor Fernández.'

Fernando quickly devoured the soup and wiped the bowl with the last piece of bread.

'Better? Paco asked.

'Much, I'm very grateful Paco. Now what do you mean, why should you be thanking me?'

'Well, the last time you came here I told you that my father had died and left me some money and I asked you how to invest it. You said, "It depends on how many Pesetas you have. If it's a large pot come and see me at my office, or if it is only modest then you might consider buying some shares in ITV Construction in Puerto de la Torre." As you said, ITV had some large contracts to build hotels, offices and apartments throughout the archipelago. Therefore, I bought some and they've done particularly well, as you know. In fact they've done so well that I think that I'll take you up on your offer to visit your office!'

'Oh that is good news; I'm very pleased for you... and me, of course!' Fernando said with a hearty laugh.

Paco got up and patted Fernando on the shoulder, 'I'll get you a coffee and leave you to gather your thoughts.'

Fernando sat and quietly berated himself for his stupidity; he had only ever gone down to Playa de los Chicos in the summertime and he had only gone there when he was younger and fitter!

Then he thought about his camera; certainly, the batteries were flat but what other damage had it sustained? The body was dirty and scratched here and there, but it seemed to be in remarkably good condition; the screen had survived and the stylus was in its slot. He just hoped that the internal memory was not damaged and that he would be able to download the images to his tower computer.

A short while later he felt ready to face the drive home.

'Right, how much do I owe you Paco?'

'Nothing Fernando, I've already told you that it is me who is in your debt. Now give me a business card and I'll make an appointment to come to see you.'

'Very well,' Fernando conceded, 'I have a card in my car. I'll do a deal with you; I'll accept your generosity only on the condition that when you come to Santa Maria, I can buy you lunch!'

They walked out to the car, '*Diablo*, I'm aching all over,' Fernando said, trying to stretch his tired limbs, 'I need to get fit, I didn't realise that I was so out of condition!'

'Well these hills are good walking country, provided you don't try to do *too* much, like hiking down to Playa de los Chicos!' Paco quipped with a grin, 'Perhaps you could go to the gym or start dance classes?'

'Huh, you're the second person to suggest that,' Fernando responded with a wry smile and he knew that it was true.

He thanked both Julia and particularly Juan for their service, shook their hands gratefully and then drove home.

On the return to his apartment, Fernando stripped himself naked, left his clothes in a pile on the kitchen floor and went to take a refreshing shower.

He kept playing over the events of the day in his mind; jumping from one recollection to another, struggling to make sense of what he had experienced.

Having dried off, he looked at himself in the mirror; the scratches on his head and face would disappear in a couple of days but the bruises to his arms and legs would take a lot longer and his right big-toe nail was a bit of mess.

Stiffly, he climbed into bed and let sleep take him.

Chapter 7 (Mon 9/3/98)

Cristobal met Alvaro on the steps of the *Iglesia de San Isidoro* in Santa Maria's central town square, both men were dressed in smart but quite casual clothes and Alvaro carried a document folder. They walked down through the park gardens and crossed the road opposite Calle García where they paused for a moment.

'Let's take a stroll up there after we've had a chat with the Harbour Master, what's his name, Pablo Méndez,' said Cristobal indicating with a nod as they ambled down to the marina.

Moored to their pontoons and floating jetties, many small yachts were bobbing at their anchorages. The bright white hulls mirrored in the clear blue of the lapping water, shoals of large fish slipped quietly between the boats whose ever-present and constant tinkling of rigging added to the ambiance; a scene of gentle serenity.

Most of the larger tourist vessels were out with their holidaymakers aboard, watching for whales and dolphins or perhaps fishing for marlin and tuna. Gulls called at each other from atop the harbour buildings, which overlooked the marina.

Pablo Méndez's office was in these buildings, which, at one time, had also housed the now-closed Customs Control. The port of Santa Maria was too small to attract any international visitors who would always make their way to the bright lights and bigger ports to the north. That was not to say that Santa Maria was a complete backwater – it was quite a bustling place - but it was sleepy compared to Puerto de la Torre!

They ascended the stairs to the first floor where Alvaro knocked on the door to the office and entered without hesitation. Pablo Méndez looked up from his desk and immediately stood. He was a short, stocky man in his late sixties with a somewhat weather-beaten complexion, his shirtsleeves were rolled up past the elbow and revealed fading tattoos on each forearm.

'I'm Captain García, *Guardia Civil*, and this is Chief Inspector Dorantes, *Cuerpo Nacional de Policía*,' announced Alvaro, extending his hand. Of course, he knew of Pablo Méndez but only in passing, their paths had never crossed directly before. The Harbour Master introduced himself, and after shaking hands with each man, indicated that they should sit down. Alvaro obliged but Cristobal sauntered over to look at the many charts, lists, and photographs, which adorned the walls of the office, which was somewhat untidy and rather dingy, mainly due to the filthy window that overlooked the harbour.

'I'd just like to confirm your statement about the unfortunate death of the Englishman at New Year.' Alvaro sorted the necessary papers from his folder and proceeded to check over what Pablo had said at the time, assuring him that it was just a formality. 'And have you thought of anything else that may be relevant?'

'No, nothing,' Pablo responded, unemotionally.

'You were not on duty that day were you, it being New Year's Day?' asked Alvaro.

'Well technically I'm always 'on duty' but, no I wasn't here until I was called, if that's what you mean,' said Pablo, quizzically.

'I see, do you have days off regularly… that is to say, days when you're not here?' Alvaro asked looking him in the eye.

'I suppose I do,' Pablo shifted in his chair, 'my wife is disabled, that's why I sold my fishing boat and took this job, so that I could be available for her needs… It's a very straightforward job you know; all of the regular vessels that come and go are just that, regulars. Visitors come and sign themselves in, if I'm not here and everything is open an above board…' he shrugged, 'except for that death, of course but that was just an unfortunate accident, wasn't it?'

Cristobal had been studying an old aerial photograph of the town that showed the old harbour and the construction of La Posada Hotel. 'Were you here on the 2nd of February?' he asked casually, without turning around.

'Um, I'm not sure…' he quickly located his desk diary amid the many papers strewn across his desk and leafed through, 'mmm no, my wife had an appointment with the chiropodist that morning…' he answered and glanced briefly at Alvaro.

Cristobal turned and smiled at Pablo, 'That's fine. Do you think that you could print off all of your logs, manifests, and registrations for all traffic in and out of the harbour, say from October last year, for every single day please? I know you've already furnished us with paperwork pertinent to this case and I know it's a big task but it would help us enormously,' he asked quietly but firmly as he walked over to the window. 'It's just that the British authorities want to be sure that we've done our job properly.' Then added casually, 'You've got a very wonderful view over the whole harbour from here, haven't you?' he mused rubbing his moustache with one hand and the window with the other.

'Oh, I see. Yes, it is a pleasant place to work; I just need to have a bit of a tidy up, sorry about the mess... I'll get all the documentation to you as soon as I possibly can gentlemen, would the end of the week be all right?' asked Pablo, slightly more at ease.

'Thank you very much,' Alvaro said sincerely as he rose, 'oh, and photocopies of your desk diary might be useful too, you never know what the British might ask for!'

'Yes certainly Captain, I'll get straight onto it.'

They each shook hands with Pablo and the two men made their way out of the building.

What do you think he's hiding, Cristobal?' Alvaro asked when they were well away from the harbour and approaching Calle García.

'Not sure... something and nothing perhaps... I wonder where he'll be on the 4th of April...' Cristobal mused, 'anyway, it looks like you'll be busy when he gets all that paperwork over to you, maybe you'll spot something.'

They crossed over the road and walked slowly along Calle García. La Posada Hotel loomed large on their left as they rounded the bend down to the rear carpark, which also gave access to the hotel's gardens. To the right, a low wall topped with a wire fence, was all that prevented access to the rocks, cliffs and sea below. Straight ahead the ground had been built up, when the hotel was erected, to allow the construction of a large swimming pool. Below were the rooms and offices of the Santa Maria Social Services; not only a meeting place for old people but also for retired sailors and fishermen. It had closed long ago when there had been a leak from the swimming pool above and new purpose built premises became available in nearby La Joya.

48

Dawdling round the carpark from the left, the men observed the gate in the wall that led up to the garden, pool and rear terraces of the hotel. A chain and padlock was holding the gate and, as Cristobal approached, he could see that both chain and lock were moderately clean and hardly showing any sign of rust or age.

They walked in silence. A few cars were parked, probably belonging to locals who were shopping, perhaps residents of the hotel or maybe anglers down on the rocks below.

As they approached the disused Social Services Offices, they slowed their pace, slightly. The fancy wrought iron window grills - *rejas* - which were once black, were now showing only a little flaking paint and much rust from the sea air. Inside, the glass windows had been covered with sheets of newspapers, which were torn, and yellowing and giving no view of the interior rooms. The main steel door into the offices was in a similar condition to the *rejas* but the handle and lock had a patina reminiscent of regular wear. A large metal roller-shutter door, big enough to admit a vehicle, was also in poor cosmetic condition but the electric operating key panel on the side wall was obviously in regular use.

Alvaro broke their silence as they drew near the wall overlooking the sea, 'Ah look Cristobal, fishermen below.'

'Indeed, I wonder if they've caught many. How do they get down there?'

'Well, as we head back up the road, at the end of the wall there,' Alvaro gesticulated ahead, 'there's a small opening and some old steps cut out of the bare rock down to the sea, it's quite precarious and there's only access to a couple of areas suitable to fish from.'

'I see, so no way to get up to the side of the old offices?' asked Cristobal quietly.

'None at all,' Alvaro responded, 'it's a sheer drop from the top pool terrace above the offices onto the rocks below which offer a natural breakwater, that's one of the reasons the developers chose this spot to build their hotel. As you know our islands are not tidal but storm surges do occur and some places suffer more than others, this is one of them, the sight of large waves crashing on the rocks is quite a spectacle for hotel residents on the seaward side.'

49

They made their way back, past the shops to the park gardens at the town square, found a shaded bench and sat down to chat.

'So the gate to the hotel gardens is used regularly, although it's locked,' said Cristobal.

'And so is the entrance and vehicular doors to the old offices,' Alvaro pronounced, 'I'll set up a discrete surveillance camera. Did you notice the dates of the old newspapers which had been used to line the windows?'

'Yes 1991 in the main.'

'Quite so, that's when the Social Services moved out.' Alvaro said, 'I would think that the interior of those rooms would be very inhospitable by now... but let's keep an open mind on that, it may simply be being used as storage for the hotel.'

Cristobal stood up and faced Alvaro, 'Very well, sort out some surveillance, see if the documents from our friend Pablo Méndez have anything to offer and I'll come over in a few days. We can examine what we have then. The Customs officer we need to have a chat with is on duty in La Joya today, so I'll go and see him. If you can have a final word with Herr Gunther and his girlfriend, that would be good. Meanwhile I have to keep the Commissioner up to date.'

By Monday morning, Fernando's slumber had refreshed him, however his aches and bruises were even more pronounced but at least his mind was clear. So taking his breakfast and coffee out onto the balcony, he proceeded to log the activity in the marina. Now he found himself paying much more attention to what direction the vessels approached the harbour; as usual, none were from the north.

With a soft cloth, he wiped the dirt from the Nikon, located its serial lead, CD-ROM driver disc and instruction manual and dropped them into his briefcase. Then he remembered that he would have to buy some new batteries on his way to the office.

He received a few odd looks and questions from various shop staff and customers about his facial scratches; one asked whether he had been overzealous whilst pruning his bougainvillea, another wondered if a new pet cat was involved and one even asked if he had been in a fight.

Things did not improve when he got to his office; when Simon saw him, he was shocked but Fernando cut him short with a brief outline of his hike, explaining that it was merely a keep-fit exercise.

'There are better ways you know,' Simon taunted, 'you could try the gym or maybe...'

'Dance classes? Yes, yes I know,' Fernando retorted, 'I'll think about it,' and sidled off into his office.

His first thought was to get the camera powered up and load the pictures onto his computer, rather than checking the state of the stock markets! With Windows 95 booted up on his computer, he slipped the CD-ROM into the drive and installed the Nikon View software. It took a few minutes, during which time he had inserted the new batteries and switched on the camera.

Using the Nikon's stylus he located the images stored in the scratch drive, connected the serial lead and selected Port COM 1 on the computer. He tapped the maximum data transfer rate on the screen and the download button in the Nikon View program, then waited for the images to be transferred, which took a while.

The first few pictures were the ones he had taken when he had purchased the camera the previous October and were mainly from around his apartment. Then came the ones he had been waiting for, Playa de los Chicos and all the litter on the ledge. 'Not bad,' he thought, 'if I'd taken a 35mm film cartridge in to be developed and printed I would still be waiting here next week!' He loaded his Epson Stylus Photo printer with glossy paper and on the computer selected all the images then sent them to print. Knowing that it would take a long time to print all the pictures, he got on with his proper job.

It was the middle of the afternoon before Fernando had a chance to look at the photographs. He discarded all of the later ones; they were simply of the track back to Fuente Armarga but he had to keep the one of his startled face when he had accidentally blinded himself and put it in his desk drawer, along with the pictures of his apartment.

He had selected the pictures to print at postcard size. The photographs that he considered to be of relevance to Alvaro and Cristobal he put to one side. The ones that Fernando deemed of most importance he reprinted at A4 size. He studied them carefully on the computer screen, zooming in on any detail, which he believed to be worthy of closer examination. Going back to the thumbnail images, he selected several, slid a blank CD-R into the computer's disc-drive and sent the shots to burn on the CD, which he would give to Alvaro later.

Chapter 9 (Mon 9/Mar/98)

The issue of placing a hidden camera in Calle García had thrown up a number of questions and problems for Alvaro. If the old offices were being used for illicit purposes, it could be that there may be a camera inside looking out! Alternatively, perhaps there were others watching the area maybe from the hotel or another building? Alvaro knew that he must consider all the possibilities and not jeopardise the operation. He could not get an operative to place a camera, however small, anywhere in the area without compromise. No, the only thing for it would be non-static, rolling observation. There certainly were not enough officers at his disposal for regular patrols and, in any case, they could not keep that up indefinitely without being noticed. Vehicles would be the only option; one parked overnight by what must look like a local resident would be easy. Maybe different vehicles throughout the daytime from commercial vans to privately owned cars of commuters, shoppers or anglers. There would be gaps as there could be no way they could manage continual or accurate recording, but surely they would get enough intelligence? Alvaro hoped so and had made the necessary arrangements.

After a few days, he had built up a clear picture in his mind of the comings and goings in the marina, having spent many hours poring over the accounts from Pablo Méndez and Fernando. He had also had a final conversation with Herr Gunther and his girlfriend before their winter sojourn had ended, and they flew back to Germany. There was nothing else of any importance they had to offer and he signed off their testimony concerning Chris Baker's death.

*

(Thurs 12/Mar/98)

Cristobal had also filed the statement made by the Customs Officer who had attended the retrieval of Chris Baker's body; there was nothing else to pursue there. He had also driven up to Puerto de la Torre to deliver his

53

interim report to Commissioner López who, as ever, was not entirely happy with progress.

He never really hit it off with the Commissioner, who he found to be an overbearing and bigoted bully. López was about 30 years old and a somewhat greasy man who had not performed particularly well until he had married the daughter of one the island's Political Elite. The men looked at each other across an unnecessarily large desk, in López' unnecessarily large office.

'It's damned inconvenient that Baker should have cracked his head open at just the wrong time, isn't it, Chief Inspector?' López asked, pointedly, completely indifferent to Cristobal's greater age and experience.

'As you say Señor,' Cristobal kept back his misgivings over Baker's death, which played on his mind as it could have involved foul play but there was no proof. Anyway, he had been instructed by his superiors at *Unidad de Drogas y Crimen Organizado* to keep López only casually informed, 'I was his back-up, but we do have some leads to follow.' He also kept Fernando's involvement clandestine from López and the UDYCO.

'Well get onto it man, I want this smuggling business tied up as soon as possible!'

'We can only work our small part in this operation Señor. As you know, I've been seconded by UDYCO and we are necessarily constrained by the EDU. I will continue to liaise with Captain Alvaro García in Santa Maria so that, as and when the EDU decide that it is the right time for international action, we will be ready.' Cristobal stated calmly.

López raised himself and slapped both hands down on the desk, 'Now look here Dorantes,' he hissed through gritted teeth, 'I don't want this crap fouling up my career, keep it tidy, understood?'

Cristobal stood up to attention and replied, 'Perfectly Commissioner, I'll keep you up to date.' He saluted and left the room. '*Tonto, jefazo, archipámpano,*' he thought to himself.

Taking a few deep breaths on the way back to his car he decided to drive straight to Santa Maria, at least he could have a sensible conversation with Alvaro!

*

The rolling surveillance in Calle García had been progressing and although some footage was poor, much had been useful. In particular, the night-time recordings yielded some interesting viewing. Alvaro had built a small team of trusted *Guardias* whose past work involved this type of activity, they were happy to watch and collate without requiring full knowledge of the motive.

Alvaro was studying one of the video tapes in his office when he was joined by Cristobal.

'Good afternoon Alvaro, anything of any consequence?'

Alvaro looked up from his computer monitor, 'well, I'm not sure about whether it's important, come and look,' he turned the display so that both men could see it, 'here; I've got a few video snips for you to view...' Cristobal pulled up a chair and Alvaro proceeded to show the clips.

All of the shots looked directly at the front of the old offices and were during the hours of darkness, luckily, streetlights gave sufficient illumination. The first video showed two men coming into shot from the left and heading directly to the door, one man had a key and as soon as the door was unlocked both men looked over their shoulders and quickly entered, closing the door behind them. Alvaro rolled the monochrome footage back then stopped it at when the men looked around; the still image was quite good.

'The fellow with the key is Miguel Moreno, La Posada Hotel manager, I don't recognise the other but one of my team says that he is sure it's a fisherman from Choco del Carmen...'

'Very well, please print a close-up of him and I'll get onto that. Hmm, what's the date and time there... ah, 1.23a.m. 11:03:1998... it's odd that no lights seem to go on in the windows... anything else?'

'Yes, have a look at them when they come out...' Alvaro said, as he searched further along the timeline, '...here, twenty minutes later, what do you make of this?' He slowed the playback down to half speed and stopped it when both men had emerged from the doorway.

Cristobal looked at Alvaro, and asked, 'Are those...'

'...Lobster pots?' They said in unison.

'It might be innocent Cristobal they could be restocking the restaurant...?'

'Yes, if the other individual turns out to be the chef, maybe, but at one-thirty in the morning? It looks a bit suspicious to me,' Cristobal mused whilst rubbing his moustache, 'any daytime activity?'

'Nothing at all that we have on camera.'

'All right, please keep watching. I think that you should have a word with the hotel's manager, he might be perfectly innocent… but he may not be. If I turn up he might think it a bit questionable but you could talk to him casually…You could say that a resident has made a complaint about something and just do a bit of digging.' Cristobal suggested.

'I've already got one of my men having a look at the records to see if anything has previously arisen, either to do with the hotel in general or Señor Moreno in particular. I'll come up with something to go and have a chat with him about.' Alvaro said whilst printing off the picture from the video recording.

'*Gracias* Alvaro. Right, I'll get back to my office and see if I can locate this fellow.'

*

After a quick call to the *Policía Local*, Alvaro found the perfect excuse to visit Miguel Moreno; he would accompany a Local Officer who was investigating a complaint about a fight, which took place at the hotel. In fact, complaints about arguments and occasional fighting were well documented, especially between certain holidaymakers. The usual course of events was that some tourists would place their bathing towels on sunbeds around the swimming pool, well before breakfast-time, thus preventing anyone else from enjoying the facility throughout the day. This was against Hotel policy but was not policed by their staff and both of these actions served to infuriate other holidaymakers' sense of 'fair play'. The friction thus created would regularly turn into large-scale quarrels and sporadic fights. Therefore, inaction by the hotel management gave Alvaro a chance to put pressure on the manager in order to test him.

Chapter 10 (Fri 13/3/98)

Alvaro and his colleague, Inspector Vicente Ibarra from the *Policía Local*, entered the hotel's front foyer and approached the reception desk. It was a very large and airy lobby; immediately opposite the reception stood a great and imposing marble stairway, which led to the other floors. To the left was a bar and lounge area, whereas to the right were lifts and a wide corridor to the dining room and restaurant. Beyond the reception was access to the rear gardens and swimming pool.

Vicente took the lead and asked the receptionist for the manager. As he was in uniform, the receptionist immediately pressed the intercom to call for Moreno who appeared from the back office within a few seconds.

A handsome man of thirty-eight, he was slimmer than the video showed him to be and he sported short, neatly cropped black hair and stubble-encrusted face. He wore a dark suit with a white shirt and understated tie, the epitome of corporate managerial staff.

He was the son of hoteliers in the large port of Algeciras but why he had not continued in the family business was not documented and he had no criminal record for Alvaro to scrutinise. All he could find out was that Moreno had been manager of La Posada for just over a year.

Introductions dispensed with, Moreno escorted them to a quiet corner of the lounge, which overlooked the rear terrace and swimming pool.

'Señor Moreno,' began Vicente, 'you're aware of the complaints which have been made about rowdiness in this establishment and in particular the fight which broke out recently. Firstly, I would like to know what steps are being taken to reduce these incidents. Secondly, is there anything which I or any of my associates,' he gave a slight nod in Alvaro's direction, 'can do to assist you?'

'Thank you gentlemen,' Moreno began, 'I'm afraid it is a deep-seated and perennial problem which affects most resorts, both here and throughout the holiday areas of Europe, as you know. That is not to say that I'm complacent about it; we have tried a few different approaches to address the issue, specifically in the education of our guests but to no avail. Of course, what might work at one hotel may not be effective in another. Even so, I have employed two guards to maintain security. The use of such guards has worked in other establishments; I'm currently trying to create a rota. There would be times when neither would be working, or only one of them and at other times both would be operational.'

'That sounds like a positive move Señor,' Vicente said, 'my job here is to help everyone as much as I can, so if there's any advice that I can give, please ask.'

'Thank you inspector, I appreciate your concern.'

'I believe that you used to work at a hotel in Algeciras, how did you deal with this sort of problem there?' Alvaro probed.

Looking straight at Alvaro, Moreno replied, 'It wasn't an issue as the accommodation was mainly for Merchant Seamen, not holidaymakers.'

'So this type of hotel management is new to you?' Alvaro asked pointedly.

'I graduated with a diploma in hospitality Captain,' Moreno bristled slightly, 'to me, managing this hotel poses no more difficulties than any other.'

'I see, what made you take this job?' Alvaro asked, pushing a little further.

'I decided that I needed a new challenge,' Moreno stiffened a little more.

'Oh, so this job *is* more challenging? You just intimated that running this hotel was no more problematic than your last one.'

'No, no you misunderstand,' Moreno softened as if he had resolved an internal quarrel, 'I mean that a new horizon beckoned.'

'While we're here, would it be too much trouble for you to let us have a full list of your employees' names and addresses, including your new security guards, please?' Alvaro asked, moving the object of his interrogation but keeping pressure on the manager.

Moreno was impassive to this new line of questioning, 'Yes of course Captain but why would you need it?'

'Because if there were any further issues, we would know who the members of staff are and who the tourists are. We wouldn't want any perpetrators of any crimes managing to fly back home without facing the law, now would we?' Alvaro replied immediately putting the manager on the back-foot again.

'I understand I can do that now. I'll get my assistant to run off a copy from the payroll.'

The three men walked back over to the reception area where Moreno barked his orders to his assistant. Alvaro casually wandered over to the glazed door that led to the pool terrace, where all of the sunbeds were occupied. He turned to see that Moreno was handing the paperwork to Vicente.

Alvaro strode back over, smiled and asked, 'Do you serve non-residents in your restaurant Señor Moreno?'

'Yes we do, why do you ask?' Moreno queried.

'Oh, my wife has a birthday soon and I thought that I could bring her here for dinner. How's your seafood?'

'Yes, of course we can accommodate you and your wife, our seafood is as good as any in Santa Maria!'

'I'll ask her when it's convenient. Are you married?'

'No I'm not; I enjoy my freedom too much!' Moreno replied with a hint of sarcasm.

Vicente and Alvaro thanked the manager for his time and took their leave.

*

By the end of the week, Fernando was still not sure of the relevance of his findings, so he collated the photographs with his weekly log of the activity at the marina and called Alvaro.

'Good day Alvaro, how are you?'

'I'm fine *gracias*, how about you?'

'Very well *gracias*. Now I have some information which you and Cristobal may find interesting... nothing to do with the harbour but a jaunt that I undertook last weekend... you may dismiss it but I do think that we should meet to discuss it, say tomorrow, Saturday 14th?' asked Fernando.

'Er, yes my diary is empty I'll check with Cristobal and get back to you. I think that we may have some bits of interest for you too...' responded Alvaro.

'Oh, right, I'm free all day so just let me know what time to expect you, if Cristobal is available.'

'Will do, talk later.'

Chapter 11 (Sat 14/3/98)

The three men were all sitting on Fernando's balcony just before noon, sipping coffee and enjoying the view. Fernando's facial blemishes were healing well, nevertheless they demanded an explanation and so he recounted his musings and self-proposed mission of the previous weekend. He deliberately kept the last couple of hours of his hike to himself as he did not think that his rescue by Paco's son to be at all relevant!

With a map of the local area spread across the table, Fernando pointed out the road to Fuente Armarga and the route of the ravine down to Playa de Los Chicos.

'You see *caballeros*, Los Chicos is completely hidden from view; the beach can only be seen from a very narrow angle out at sea. Perhaps it's just a coincidence that the newspaper, *La Hoja Informativa*, is dated the third of March...' Fernando said, 'But the whole situation there is somewhat suspicious, don't you think?'

'I think you're quite right,' said Cristobal, rubbing his moustache, 'someone has certainly been using the place as a view-point... We could send a forensics team there but that may alert any criminals...'

Alvaro was leafing through the other of Fernando's pictures and proffered one in particular to Cristobal, 'what do you make of this?' he asked, 'down on the beach...'

Cristobal scrutinised the detail and looked up at Alvaro and Fernando in turn, 'lobster pots...' he stated simply, 'it could be innocent, we could do with knowing who has a license to fish in that area, leave that with me, but I take your point.'

Fernando was curious about the cryptic exchange between the other two and it was not lost on Cristobal.

'We have another line of enquiry concerning lobster pots, *amigo*, here look at this photo,' Cristobal searched through his own documents and passed the picture of Miguel Moreno, the Posada Hotel manager with another man and lobster pot, which had been taken from the surveillance camera, to Fernando who looked at it blankly.

61

Alvaro cut in and explained how the picture had been obtained, 'so there may be a link with your picture and ours, we need to know who the other man is, though…'

'Ah, well I've had one of my team on that,' said Cristobal, 'and we have found him; Manolo Ruiz has his own boat, *El Alborán* based in Choco del Carmen, keeps to himself, is said to be a wife-beater - but we have no proof of that. Apparently he does occasionally take people out for Marlin and Tuna fishing trips…' he looked directly at Fernando, 'how are your sea-legs?'

'What…? Who, me…?' Fernando hesitated, '…oh, I get it, and you want me to check him out?'

'Yes please, if we sent one of our officers I'm sure that Ruiz would spot him straight away,' answered Cristobal.

'Well, it's been a while since I was on board a boat but I'll have a go, it's a little too early in the season for Marlin but Tuna will be around… I wonder how much he charges…' he said, looking directly back at Cristobal.

'No idea and we don't have an expense account for it sorry, you'll just have to get out there and enjoy it *amigo*,' Cristobal said with a grin.

Fernando raised his eyes heavenward and sighed, 'All right I'll take a reconnaissance walk over there.'

'Well, if we're right about all this, the next shipment will be three weeks today, 4th April at 10a.m.,' Alvaro said, looking up from his paperwork, 'and don't forget that the clocks go forward two weeks tomorrow, 29th…'

'Right,' said Fernando, 'I'll go this afternoon and again tomorrow if necessary, with a view to getting a trip next weekend.' His decisiveness caused Cristobal and Alvaro to nod favourably to each other.

'I must say Fernando, we're very grateful for your efforts here and I know it must go against your naturally cautious nature, *gracias*,' said Cristobal, appreciatively.

'I know… it's a bit of a surprise to me too! Of course, I could be having a mid-life crisis! But seriously, I'm happy to help,' Fernando said, looking Cristobal and Alvaro in the eye, 'it's given me a different perspective on things; I don't like what is going on in Santa Maria. I don't like to think about the misery that drug addiction causes, let alone organised crime bosses undermining the lives of ordinary hard working people - like me. On the other hand it *is* giving employment to people like you!'

'That's true!' Cristobal laughed, 'I'm glad you're with us in this though.'

Fernando handed his marina observations, CD and photographs to Alvaro and Cristobal who took their leave.

'Right,' thought Fernando, carefully folding the picture of Manolo Ruiz and putting it in his pocket, 'I'm going to walk down into town, past Isla de los Cangrejos and Los Roques then on to Choco Del Carmen. If I can walk to Los Chicos from Fuente Armarga and back, I can manage this.' Nevertheless, he put on some sturdy walking shoes and casual outdoor clothes and took his camera before striding off. 'I wonder what Amanda would make of all this? He thought, as he closed the apartment door.

The first part of the walk from his apartment block was the steepest downhill stretch - the bit that was always worst coming back up! He looked briefly at his parked car then back to the road. After rounding to the left, the roadway boasted a pavement and spectacular views over the town. Small houses with well-kept gardens and steep driveways took his attention; when driving he was necessarily only aware of the road.

Just a slow incline for perhaps seven or eight minutes and he came to the junction; to his right he could continue down into town, or left to the main road and *autovia* to other parts of the island but he chose the road directly opposite, to the roundabout *La Glorieta*. There was quite a lot of traffic going to and from the town; both vehicular and pedestrian but it was Saturday afternoon. The roadway to the roundabout was flat with paving on both sides and flanked by small, low-rise apartment blocks surrounded by palm trees, with well-kept gardens of oleander and hibiscus.

By the time Fernando had reached *La Glorieta,* a garden oasis framed by the dark grey asphalt road, he had only been walking for about fifteen minutes and he felt pleased with himself, although he still wasn't looking forward to the return journey! He tried to convince himself of the therapeutic effect that the exercise would have.

Bearing right at the traffic island, he stopped to look at the impressive, steep gully, strewn with boulders carried by thankfully rare flash floods coming from higher up the mountain and down to the sea. The coast was probably no more than five hundred metres away but maybe five hundred metres below where he stood looking.

There was virtually no traffic as he continued down to Isla de los Cangrejos with its fabulous private gate-fronted villas. He paused and considered the cost of the properties; he had several clients from the development and wondered if life there might be for him? Turning and looking up he could see the pink, white and burgundy bougainvillea tumbling over his balcony way up above the town. No, he would keep his apartment; the expansive villas before him were no match for his demesne!

Fernando estimated that he was probably at the halfway point in his journey as he passed Los Cangrejos. The going was easy and the villas petered out and gave way to barren rock and shrub-land; one day some enterprising developer would build there, thought Fernando but not too far from the road as Los Roques, as it was called, was full of caves, half-flooded lava tubes and dangerous rocky inlets.

The approach to Choco Del Carmen was picturesque as the road made its way down to the small fishing village. Fernando could see the white terraced houses, their blue painted doors and window frames, cheek-by-jowl tiered down on either side of the steep cliffs to the narrow inlet with its very small black-sand beach.

Sheltered from south, north and north-west, the village was well positioned to weather all but the very worst of stormy seas, which were mercifully infrequent.

Hewn out of the cliffs on the northern face of the bay, the harbour had many small boats moored along its one hundred and fifty metre length.

A few people were about; some tourists enjoying an al fresco drink at the small bars and cafés along the waterfront, fishermen busy with maintenance and preparation for setting sail aboard their boats and local people going about their business. Fernando strolled slowly along, casually but intently looking at each boat, searching for *El Alborán* and Manolo Ruiz.

It was not long before Fernando located his quarry. The monochrome photo, which Cristobal had given to him, did not do justice to Ruiz; he was tall for a Spaniard, muscular and had a somewhat mean and swarthy countenance. He was busy hosing down lobsterpots and stacking them on the quayside by his boat.

'Good day, Manolo Ruiz?' called Fernando as he approached.

'Good day, yes, what can I do for you?' Ruiz responded.

'I'm Fernando,' he said extending his hand, which the fisherman shook, firmly, 'I was chatting with some lads in Santa Maria recently, they recommended that you may be able to take me out to do a bit of Tuna fishing?'

'Oh yes, who were they?' the fisherman asked quizzically.

'Er, I'm not sure, we were just chatting over a coffee, you know how it is! Anyway I haven't been fishing since my boys left home, we used to go out, when they were young, with old Pablo Méndez but he retired a couple of years ago. And hey, look at me' he said slapping his paunch, 'I could do with getting a bit of fitness back! Do you think it's something you could help me with?'

'Well, I charge the same rate for locals as I do for tourists,' he said flatly, 'you know there are better ways to get fit; you could go to a gym or go dancing with your wife?'

Fernando groaned inwardly, 'She died and neither of those activities is very appealing or exciting.'

Ruiz shrugged, 'Okay, when are you free? We could go out this afternoon, if you like?'

'Yes all right,' Fernando shocked himself with his response and felt a surge of adrenaline course through his body, 'I was just going for a long walk but what the hell, *vamos!*'

El Alborán was a traditional fishing boat; mainly white with blue detail, a central wheelhouse with radio, sonar and radar. It would probably not be a match for the modern high-speed boats, which were becoming more popular with the tourists, thought Fernando.

Ruiz prepared the vessel for departure, beckoned Fernando aboard, and offered him a pair of rubber boots.

After casting off, Fernando was rather surprised when Ruiz started to open up the engine; he had expected a '*phut-phut-phut*' but was greeted with more of a throaty V-8 type of 'growl'. Ruiz reduced the power slightly, so that they stayed within the harbour speed limit as Fernando made his way from the stern toward the wheelhouse and proceeded to take mental notes of the boat's particulars. The electronic equipment looked a lot more sophisticated than Pablo Mendez' but perhaps that was just progress, thought Fernando.

Leaving Choco Del Carmen, they rounded Los Roques to the north and had a perfect view of the Cuevas, 'I guess it was in one of those caves that those poor teenagers drowned a few years ago...' Fernando said flatly to Ruiz.

'Yes and that's despite the warnings and signage there, look.' Ruiz answered dramatically and pointed to a large but weather-beaten hoarding declaring: CUEVAS PELIGROSO POSIBILIDAD DE MUERTE, (dangerous caves, possibility of death). 'It only takes a small swell and... well, you know... it's all magnified; a wave enters one of those lava tubes and it's a maelstrom, crushing bathers against the sides and tops, sometimes preventing even the strongest swimmers from getting back out... And all sorts of crap gets washed up in there not to mention the Congers and Morays...'

Fernando looked intently at the scene as they sailed past. Since the tragedy, an attempt had been made to put bars across some of the smaller cave entrances but like the large sign, the sea and weather had taken their toll. He quickly switched on his Nikon and took a few snaps, 'for the album,' he said to Ruiz who was looking directly at him, 'and if we catch any fish I can send pictures of them too, on to my sons, they'll love it!' he said with an excited grin on his face. However, he had to glance at the caves again to confirm that he had just glimpsed a pink buoy, bobbing deep within one of the larger caves, but it was gone.

Ruiz turned the wheel to port, took a course due west and opened up the throttle; if Fernando had not been steadying himself to the gunwale he would have been thrown aft.

Less than ten minutes later, Ruiz slowed the boat to only a few knots and turned due north. He locked the throttle and fixed their course, then busied himself setting five rods into their fixed housings astern. Meanwhile Fernando had been enjoying the view of Santa Maria, east of their position. They were still a lot closer to his hometown than to the island of La Goma, perhaps about two kilometres out. The buildings of the town were visible but he could not pick out his apartment with any certainty, now he wished he had brought his binoculars.

'Hey *hombre*, that's the bait box,' said Ruiz, pointing to an insulated cupboard by the wheelhouse, 'be ready to pass some fish when I say.' Ruiz was busy tying lures and hooks to the rod lines. When Fernando opened the bait box, he was not quite ready for the strength of the fishy stench that assailed his nostrils! 'Okay, pass one over,' said Ruiz, 'oh, there's a bucket and line next to the bait box, drop it overboard and get some seawater, don't bother with the hose, the pump is broken.'

Fernando handed the dead fish to Ruiz, grabbed the bucket, slung it over the side to fill with water and then proceeded to wash his hands.

'Here, you take these two rods,' said Ruiz, 'I'll have the others.'

Fernando played the lines out and they both waited.

After a few minutes, Ruiz checked their heading and adjusted the speed. Fernando noticed how precisely the fisherman made the fine alterations to his boat and how composed he was in spite of the swell.

'So, you know about me, how do you fill your days?' asked Ruiz bluntly.

Fernando hadn't lied so far and didn't want to now, 'Oh, I work as a consultant in a finance office – really boring – tax and all that sort of stuff,' he said with an upward nod of his head, 'hey, I'm on...!' Fernando grabbed his rod to steady it in one hand and began to reel in gently.

'Slowly now,' said Ruiz, 'ah, I can see that you've done this before…' and continued to encourage with; 'that's it, keep it going like that… tire him out… really good… keep going…'

At length, they could see the silver flashes from the flanks of the Bluefin.

'That's it, hold him there, watch now, he'll start circling slowly… he has no energy left… he's ready… I'll get the gaff.'

By now, Fernando had the line as short as he could with the fish just below the surface of the water on the starboard side. Ruiz leaned over the gunwale with his gaff and waited patiently for the tuna to be in just the right position.

Without ceremony, he struck and hauled-out in one swift, clean and decisive arc bringing the fish aboard. Immediately he had his boot on the tail and held the head down with the gaff. Reaching into his pocket, he produced a T-shaped tool, the top in his palm and a pointed rod slipping out between his forefinger and middle. Locating a spot between the eyes he plunged the point in and back to the brain. The tuna convulsed and it was all over, or so Fernando thought; Ruiz removed the gaff and hook, and then slid a large switchblade out of his boot. His knife was clearly sharp, he dug it into the side of the tuna and twisted, just a few centimetres back from the gills behind the pectoral fin, and blood gushed out profusely. He turned the fish over and stuck the blade in again, more blood, 'get the bucket,' he commanded, 'and sluice down.' Fernando did as he was ordered and as he refilled the bucket, he watched Ruiz cut a wedge shaped chunk out of the tuna, just behind the head.

Fernando was now witnessing something he had not seen before; he could see that Ruiz had exposed the top of the spine. Throwing the wedge overboard there were several gulls all screeching as they flew about the boat and dove in for one of them to retrieve the meat.

Now Ruiz produced a thin wire perhaps twenty centimetres long and slid it down inside the tuna's spine to displace the chord. The fish flailed about as he slid the wire in and out, 'don't worry, he's dead, that will relax the meat, look,' Fernando watched in amazement as Ruiz prodded the side of the fish the meat of which was now quite soft and pliable, 'about fifteen kilos, I'd say.'

Ruiz retrieved his knife, slid the tip expertly into the belly, and carefully cut forward to below the gills. Lifting the gills on one side, he cut deftly in behind and round, turned the fish over and did the same to the other side, a little more severing and he pulled out the gills, guts and heart which he threw over his shoulder for the gulls.

The fisherman was extremely confident in his actions, a master of his trade. But he also emanated an air of menace; he could probably dispatch a man just as ruthlessly, he was a dangerous individual and Fernando could feel it.

'We're on again Captain!' shouted Fernando.

'Do what you did before and you'll be fine!' called Ruiz from the wheelhouse from where he was collecting a couple of large cool-bags and pre-packaged ice from his freezer. Half-filling one bag with ice, he stuffed more ice in the tuna's body cavity, put the fish in the bag, covered it with the ice, topped up with water, and then zipped up the bag.

'Damn it! I forgot to take some pictures, if we land this one…' Fernando said through gritted teeth as he began to reel in. He need not have reproached himself as a repeat performance played out but this time on the port side and he remembered to take some photographs.

After packing the second fish in ice, Ruiz turned the boat about, opened up the throttle and set a course home. Fernando glanced about and realised that they were as far north as Playa de los Chicos but too far from the coast to see the tiny beach, but he took more pictures anyway. They journeyed in silence and it was not until they were near Punta Piqueña that Fernando realised they were heading for Santa Maria.

'Are we not going back to Choco Del Carmen?' asked Fernando.

'No, Santa Maria is where you live, I assume? I'm not sure you'd be able to walk back from Choco with two tunas!' Ruiz retorted.

'Oh, that's great thank you! But I don't need or want both of them! Don't you want one?'

'Well, yes I can sell on to one of the seafood restaurants…' Ruiz responded.

'I must say I've had a really good time, I'd forgotten how exciting it can be, thank you Captain Ruiz.'

69

Fernando was taking special notice of the course they were on as they approached the harbour; this was a different perspective to the one from his balcony! He took more photographs.

At last, Ruiz drew the boat along the waterfront, allowing Fernando to climb out with the bow rope and tie off to a mooring ring. Ruiz manoeuvred the vessel alongside and threw out the stern rope.

'It's amazing, I haven't done any of this for probably ten years but it's obviously all there, locked in the back of my mind, muscle-memory, I suppose,' Fernando said as he tied the last hitch. That was when it struck him again; the gulls were still all around hoping for a morsel or tit-bit thrown from the boat! They had followed along all the way back to Santa Maria! His mind flashed back to what he had seen on New Year's Day; only a boat *with* fish would have gulls, a boat *without* fish would have *no* gulls!

Ruiz had emptied all of the ice out of one bag, replaced the tuna inside and handed it to Fernando. He only half emptied the other bag of ice; it would weigh heavy but he only planned to carry it to the marina restaurants. If none of them were interested, he would try his hand in Choco Del Carmen and if no luck there, he would take it home.

'I'd like to do that again, in due course, if that's possible Captain?' Fernando asked as they walked along towards the town.

'Yes all right, you'll have to take pot-luck though, you were lucky today, I never really know where I'll be, or when!' Ruiz responded cryptically.

'I'll bring the bag back when I see you next. Do you have a phone?'

'No point,' Ruiz said dryly, 'the signal here is poor but non-existent in Choco!'

'Fair enough, good point. Well thank you for a most enjoyable afternoon, I hope to see you again soon, *adios*.' Ruiz grunted a response and made his way to the restaurants.

Fernando pondered as he plodded up to the centre of town, 'then what was that I saw by Ruiz's radar, a satellite phone, perhaps?

He looked up to his apartment; the weight of the fish was beginning to tell on his shoulder, 'no way am I walking all the way back up there with this!' he thought to himself and hailed a passing taxi.

The day had slipped into night without Fernando noticing, he automatically switched on the lights and went straight to his kitchen. After locating a clean bucket, he poured in a large amount of salt and filled it with water to make brine, which he needed for washing down.

The cool-bag required a good wash if it were to be used again, which was his first job. Then he located his filleting knife, which he immediately sharpened.

With a chopping board on his counter-top, Fernando set about his catch, continuing the work started by Manolo Ruiz. First, he removed the head, then the tail. He decided on two top and two lower fillets, back loins and belly loins.

Amanda never wanted to be a party to the catching or filleting of fish but she had loved to eat it!

Twenty minutes later and he was ready to vacuum pack the steaks. Years ago, Fernando would have made a nice stock with some of the leftovers but this time he could not be bothered, now they were double-bagged and in the rubbish bin.

He had kept one steak back and as he put the remainder in his 'fridge, he got out an onion, tomato and some lettuce leaves. A dash of olive oil in his griddle-pan to sear the tuna and he sat down to one of the best meals he had cooked in a long time!

After his repast, Fernando had a quick shower and put on some clean clothes, the day was not done yet and he switched on his computer. His camera had proved its worth again and he downloaded all of the day's photographs. Looking at them on the monitor, he said to himself; 'Cristobal and Alvaro are going to enjoy these!'

'Alvaro, remind me again why we're going to La Posada,' asked Isabella as she applied finishing touches to her make-up, 'I know it's supposed to be my birthday but what do you hope to gain for your investigation?'

'You know that I can't tell you much,' he said whilst putting his jacket on, 'suffice to say it's a sort of general reconnaissance. I'd also like to hear what your feminine intuition has to tell you about the manager, Miguel Moreno.'

'All right, are you sure he's going to be in this evening, Wednesday could be his day off?'

'Oh he'll be in, he knows that we're going for dinner and I'm sure he'll want to keep an eye on me, just as I'll be watching him!' Alvaro stated frankly.

Isabella was wearing a light, low cut floral dress, which showed off her attractive décolletage. She also had a plain shawl over her arm and her heels were nearly high enough to bring her up to Alvaro's height. He had chosen to wear slate coloured Chinos, tan espadrilles, a white open-neck shirt and a light tan jacket. They looked a most striking and confident couple as they strolled into the lobby of the hotel and up to the reception desk.

Moreno was in conversation with the receptionist but broke off abruptly upon seeing Alvaro and Isabella.

'Captain García, good evening,' Moreno said making his way round to them. The men shook hands and Alvaro introduced his wife. Moreno offered his hand to Isabella, '*Encantada*,' he said whilst slowly dipping his head allowing his eyes to wonder from her face down to her cleavage, 'happy birthday Señora García, allow me to show you to the restaurant.'

Approaching the check-in, Moreno beckoned to the Maître d'hôtel, exchanged a few quiet words with him, turned and bowed to Alvaro and Isabella who indicated their thanks and followed the Maître d' who led them to their table.

Alvaro had specifically asked to be seated on the balcony, which had a view of the sea, and he was not disappointed. From their table he could see into the restaurant, across the gardens and most importantly down to the old offices below the swimming pool. Isabella could see from the gardens to the marina and the towering cliffs running away to the north. It was a romantic scene; the couple were bathed in the golden glow of the sunset to the west as they looked out and held hands across the table.

Alvaro looked directly at Isabella and she turned to look at him, a faint smile played on his lips, then he whispered, 'I love you, you do know that don't you?'

Isabella smiled and responded, 'And I love you too.'

They were interrupted by the Sommelier who was carrying a bottle of Cava, an ice bucket and two flutes. Alvaro and Isabella looked at him with a questioning gaze. 'With the compliments of the manager Señor, happy birthday Señora,' he said as he proceeded to pop the cork and pour the foaming wine into the two glasses.

'That's very kind, *gracias*,' said Alvaro.

'*De nada* Señor, here is the wine list for your perusal. I'll return to you once you have decided on your preferences from this evening's dinner menu.'

With a smile, Alvaro nodded his affirmation and the Sommelier returned to his station.

'That's most thoughtful of him,' commented Isabella, 'but I bet the sceptic in you has another view!'

'Yes, I'm afraid that Moreno is trying to keep me sweet, at the same time being a little over gallant to you!' Alvaro raised his flute and said, '*Amorcita, sabes que te quiero mucho.*' Isabella followed with, '*igualmente amorcito.*' They touched glasses and saluted each other.

'I know that you've only met him briefly but what does your intuition tell you?' Alvaro asked quietly.

'Well, he's certainly handsome! However, I suspect he's a bit of a womaniser, unmarried and happy to keep it that way! I wouldn't trust him!' Isabella responded raising her eyebrows and inclining her head to one side. 'What do you think of him?'

'I don't know about the 'handsome' part but you're right, he's not married,' Alvaro chuckled softly, 'and I don't trust him either!'

They chatted quietly for a short while before the waiter returned for their orders.

Alvaro asked for lobster and showed only mild disappointment when the waiter said that they had none, whilst his mind began to work overtime on the possible implications.

Their meals were served to them in an unhurried but timely manner, giving them the opportunity to observe the comings and goings both inside and outside the restaurant, as they watched the sun set.

Alvaro calculated that it would take less than a minute for someone to exit the offices below the pool and be up into the hotel, including unlocking and relocking the gate, then climbing the steps to the terrace. He made a mental note to check if the original building plans for the hotel were still held in the Town Hall, it could be interesting to see the 'below stairs' layout; service corridors, elevators, etc.

When the waiter returned to remove the last of the plates, Alvaro asked for the bill and when it arrived, it was with two small complimentary Soberano Reserva Brandies.

They toasted one another and sipped the spirit as they looked out over the floodlit gardens.

When it came time to leave, Alvaro paid the bill and asked the Maître d'hôtel to thank the staff and management for their evening but Moreno was nowhere to be seen.

'Well, are we Dumas' Three Musketeers or Macbeth's Three Witches?' Fernando quipped as he, Cristobal and Alvaro sat in their accustomed positions on the balcony.

Alvaro smiled and Cristobal grunted in accord.

'Right, I've got nothing to report regarding the harbour but here's the paperwork anyway,' Fernando passed the documents to Alvaro, 'however, I did take a walk to Choco Del Carmen last Saturday and had a trip out with your man, Manolo Ruiz...'

Cristobal and Alvaro both turned with eyebrows raised with surprised expectancy to Fernando.

'And I hope to get out for another trip with him this afternoon, if I can, which is why I thought we'd meet a little earlier, today,' said Fernando as he produced the photographs from the voyage and proceeded to talk through the entire expedition of the previous weekend. He left nothing out, giving a full account of his experience and observations.

'So, in conclusion; Ruiz is defensive, powerfully built, has excellent coastal knowledge and can control his environment confidently. His boat is a lot more capable than it looks and has up-to-date equipment.

'Excellent work, Fernando,' said Cristobal, 'so you think you might go out again today?'

'I hope so, I really enjoyed it! And I've got some tuna for both of you, if you'd like some?'

'Yes please!' in unison, was their emphatic response.

Cristobal leaned forward a little, 'all right my friend, this time I'd like you to see if you can get a good look at that satellite phone, if possible, and anything else on the boat that might seem out of place, odd or incongruous, photographs too, if you can.'

Fernando nodded an affirmation.

'I have some news myself,' said Alvaro, 'Moreno and Ruiz were caught on camera again at around 01:30hrs last Wednesday morning...' he passed a couple of grainy pictures over, 'same as the previous week, with the lobster pots... Interestingly, a van backed up to the door to the offices late on

Monday afternoon and something was off-loaded but the camera angle from our undercover car was compromised by the van. Also, I took Isabella for a meal in La Posada on Wednesday evening... and guess what... they didn't have any lobster!'

'Oh, that's very interesting,' said Cristobal, rubbing his moustache, 'In that case, I think that we can assume that the lobster pots are just a cover...Ah now, that's given me an idea...'

Alvaro and Fernando looked at him expectantly.

Cristobal glanced at them, 'not now, there's something I need to do first...'

'Right,' said Alvaro, 'well I had a visit, yesterday, downstairs to the Town Hall Planning Department... I thought it might be useful to see the original plans for La Posada Hotel and fortunately, they were still in the archive. I made an excuse to the archivist about wanting to know about the history of Santa Maria... Anyway, they show all of the service elevators, stairs, corridors and basement rooms, including those under the swimming pool. I had assumed that those old offices were just a few odd rooms fronting onto the road but I was wrong. Far from being built directly onto the cliffs running down to the sea, the pool is on stilts, completely blocked-in on three sides, adding to the strength of the structure with the front being the only access. Therefore, the interior area is more or less the same size as the pool and terrace but with pillars, so it could be partitioned into smaller areas.

'Oh yes, the pump and filtration house is an independent separate building located at the opposite end of the pool with its own entrance.

'Now, ventilation to the under-pool area is via several airbricks, a couple at the back but mainly on the side facing the sea. You know how strong the wind around here can be and I'm sure that the air holes are vermin-proof, so it's probably quite dry in there, but no natural light beyond the offices. If you remember, the offices were closed down a few years ago, when the pool sprung a leak. The original contractors made the repair, which was a leak from one of the pool filtration skimmer pipes. Apparently, they just replaced the pipe, as they're all accessible below the pool, and resealed the whole underside with some sort of rubber latex solution. But the offices have remained closed ever since.'

'Well done Alvaro, excellent work,' commented Cristobal, 'anything about the main building worth noting?'

'Yes, as you know, the main staircase is in the centre of the building, as is reception. A second stair leads from there, outside to the pool on the lower terrace. There's also another stair from behind reception, down inside to a couple of storage rooms which also have a security door to outside, in the gardens by the pool. Not far from the access path to the road and parking, by the old offices,' Alvaro noted, 'I looked closely on Wednesday and I didn't notice a security door, so I think that it is well hidden behind shrubs and bushes and cannot be seen easily. So that would give quite covert access to and from the hotel and offices for Moreno and Ruiz.'

'Hold on,' interjected Fernando, 'so these boats coming from South America have a rendezvous with Ruiz who then brings the drugs to Moreno...what then?

'Well, put simply, yes that's what we think,' Cristobal answered, 'we have to work out how and where the meetings take place, how many people are involved and how Moreno distributes the cocaine.'

'I see,' said Fernando.

Alvaro picked up the thread, 'most likely they communicate with satellite phones and they probably meet way out at sea at different coordinates each time. Maybe Ruiz stashes the cocaine near Playa de los Chicos, perhaps elsewhere too, and then he brings it to Santa Maria on the appointed day and time. Then Moreno and Ruiz prepare the drugs, in some way, ready for further distribution.'

Cristobal followed, 'quite so, and they've been doing this unhindered, possibly for years. It's a tried and tested system that they operate, one that works well for them but that doesn't mean that they'll be complacent, far from it! The EDU know it and that is why our operation has to succeed. Now, the boarding of one of the vessels from the source will have compromised them for a while but that doesn't mean that Moreno, Ruiz, *et al* don't have some stock of the drugs, cached somewhere, in order to maintain a constant, steady supply from here. But thanks to you Fernando, were getting closer by the day. Right *caballeros*,' he addressed them both directly and abruptly, 'I have something that I want to look into,' and with that, took his leave.

Alvaro continued chatting briefly with Fernando but they too parted company.

Having decided not to have another coffee, Fernando instead prepared himself for a walk down to Choco Del Carmen, to see if he could go fishing again.

Before dressing in his outdoor gear, Fernando weighed himself; he had lost three and a half kilos since the start of the year! 'Well,' he said aloud, 'at this rate I'll reach my target by midsummer, all this activity is doing me some good!'

Stepping out onto the road, he realised he was not just excited to think that he may get some more fishing that afternoon, but he was actually looking forward to the walk to Choco. The sun shone down, and the springtime views were fresh and clear. There had been some rain in the last couple of months, at the coast, but nothing to mention. However, on the mountain, throughout winter, there had been a lot of snow. He could see the white peak of the volcano high above the nearby hills cast against the impossibly blue sky and the whole vista around made him smile. Such a pity he had no one else in his life to enjoy it too.

His pace was fast but easy and he was striding down into Choco Del Carmen in no time. He looked along the harbour for *El Alborán* but it was not there. So he turned his attention to the sea, this time he had brought his binoculars, and he scanned the water out to the north-west. His mind flashed back to New Year's Day, the first time he had seen the 'seagull-less' boat sailing into Santa Maria. He could see it now cruising in to Choco but this time with the associated gulls. There was no doubt in his mind; this was definitely the same vessel.

There was no hurry now; he strolled slowly along to the space where *El Alborán* had been moored the previous week. With nothing to do whilst the boat came in, he sat down with a soft drink at a nearby bar to wait. Hopefully Ruiz was returning from a morning's fishing and would go out again, like last weekend.

Finally, Ruiz brought the boat alongside and moored up. Four other men on board, obviously tourists, were laughing and bragging between themselves about their day's angling. They thanked Ruiz, disembarked and went on their way.

A local restauranteur strolled over to *El Alborán*; 'anything for me Manolo?' he called to Ruiz.

'Only if you take the lot,' was the short reply.

A few minutes on board, looking at the catch, haggling about the price and the deal was done. Five large ice-filled trays of fish and a bucket of lobsters were off-loaded to the quayside where an aproned chef was waiting with a hand truck.

Fernando walked over to the boat and hailed Ruiz; 'Captain, will you be going out again today?'

The fisherman looked up at Fernando, there was a moment of hesitation before recollection, 'yes, if you don't mind company.'

'Not at all. Here, I've brought your cool bag back from last week.' Fernando responded and stepped aboard.

'How's your English?' Ruiz asked bluntly and passed some rubber boots to Fernando.

'I can get by, why?'

'Those two *chavos* coming now,' Ruiz said, gesticulating to the quayside.

The couple were in their late twenties or early thirties, one dark haired the other was quite fair. They waved as they approached and Ruiz beckoned them on board, then handed them some boots in exchange for their trainers.

Fernando introduced himself and the lads gave their names: David and Mark.

'It will be wet out there and you don't want to slip,' Fernando said in his best English, 'and it looks a little bumpy, be sure you hold on,' the boys thanked him and Ruiz readied for departure.

They quietly chugged their way out to the open sea and, as Fernando had said, there was a swell. Ruiz opened the throttle and the bow rose up as they made their way to the North West. Farther out towards La Goma than previously, several Dolphins rode playfully on the vessel's bow-waves. Fernando enjoyed the spectacle. Of course he had seen dolphins before, but the English boys were really excited and took many photos' with their 35mm SLR's.

Fernando estimated that they were half way between Santa Maria to the east and La Goma to the west, when Ruiz slowed the boat and set a northerly course.

'Shall I get the bucket out Captain?' Fernando asked Ruiz.

'Yes, over there,' he pointed, 'and you'll find the hose in there too. Connect it up to the tap. I've had the pump fixed, but you need to switch it on, in the cupboard, starboard side in the wheelhouse.'

'Okay,' Fernando responded, but fortuitously he had misunderstood the instruction and went to the starboard side hold, a large stowage chamber. On opening it, he could see much diving equipment including wetsuits, masks, flippers, scuba tanks and an orange Farallon hand-held diver propulsion vehicle - an underwater scooter.

'Not there, *tonto*, in the wheelhouse!' Ruiz bellowed and pointed wildly.

Fernando slapped his own forehead with his palm and feigned stupidity, 'ah, sorry, got it,' he said. However, it did not put him off having a good glance around whilst locating the pump switch, for the satellite phone, etc. He spotted the handset in a charging cradle by the radar screen and made a mental note of it, as he could not see any possibility of getting photos'. It was a state-of-the-art Motorola Iridium with a stubby, fat antenna, altogether bigger than his own trusty old Nokia 2110 mobile phone.

David and Mark watched on as Fernando helped Ruiz to prepare and bait the fishing rods. Fernando felt strangely comfortable; almost like when he used to be out with his own lads, just those few, short years ago.

Ruiz made some small adjustments to the boat's course and speed and Fernando noticed that they were level with Playa De Los Chicos, now due east from their position. They were well out, away from the land, but through his binoculars, Fernando could make out the small beach and, more importantly, the cascade from the *embalse* by the *mirador* where he had been just thirteen days before. Again, the thought of Amanda stirred in his mind, *'there's a job to be done and it won't get finished unless you start it...'* Excitement from the stern awoke him from his reverie; there was a fish on the line.

Ruiz helped David to work the tuna and tire it out before finally landing it, then all three watched on as Ruiz despatched the fish.

'What's he doing?' Mark asked Fernando.

'Is there a name for that procedure Captain?' Fernando questioned Ruiz.

'Japanese method; *"Ike jime"*. Quick death for the fish and better for the meat!' Ruiz responded without looking up and continued the process that

Fernando had previously witnessed. He relayed the comments to the boys who nodded their understanding.

The single tuna was to be their only landed catch of the afternoon; they had lost another two, mainly due to Mark's inexperience and inability to listen to instructions. However, Fernando was satisfied, after all he had had an interesting day and had some information for Cristobal and Alvaro, such as it was. The English boys both looked a bit sea sick, due to the choppiness of the water. They were ready for the homeward journey to Choco Del Carmen. Even so, they asked Ruiz to take them out again later that week and booked the whole of Friday 26th.

The walk back for Fernando was fairly demanding, especially the last trudge from La Glorieta traffic island up to his apartment, but at least he wasn't carrying a tuna!

Chapter 16 (Sat 21/3/98)

Cristobal had his suspicions about the exportation of the drugs and had formulated a plan.

It was just after noon and he looked at himself in his bathroom mirror. He had trimmed his moustache back a couple of days earlier and not bothered to shave the previous day. No one had noticed as he usually had a five o'clock shadow at nine in the morning anyway! His natural dark complexion added to the look he was trying to achieve; a casual local, with the visage of a manual worker.

He reached into his wardrobe and selected a shirt with a small checked pattern, an old, well-worn one, which he customarily only wore when doing chores around his house. Searching through many incongruous outfits, he drew out a hanger on which hung a pair of slightly shabby trousers with light-reflective strips and a matching jacket in mid-blue heavy cotton, the type worn by working people, road workers, electricians, plumbers and mechanics, etc. A pair of plain-glass, black rimmed spectacles, peaked baseball cap, old shoes, a tool bag and his disguise was complete.

Having dressed, he certainly looked the part as the clothes were just slightly too big for him on his small frame which compounded the look of an inconsequential worker.

Rummaging in his kitchen drawer Cristobal located his laminated airport security tag. At least *that* was genuine; for the airport and coastguard enforcement services were keen to share general intelligence with the land-based *Guardia* and Police forces.

He had called the Chief of the Customs Surveillance Service (*Servicio de Vigilancia Aduanera*, SVA) Juan Rodriguez, his colleague at the airport, saying that he might be visiting, incognito at some point, vaguely suggesting that he was investigating a domestic kidnapping. Nevertheless, he took his *Guardia* identity as well, in case he was challenged.

Forty minutes later, he arrived at the International Airport Staff Car Park. He then casually made his way to the main entrance, where many coaches were busy dropping off holidaymakers for their return flights to Northern Europe.

Cristobal stood aside and watched the crowd of people as they jostled one another for their luggage. Alvaro had furnished him with details of La Posada coaches coming to and from the hotel and airport, with coach numbers and final destinations.

He moved around the entrance and concourse, watching casually but intently from a distance, for several hours. Patterns emerged of coaches arriving, emptying, and then driving on to arrivals and passengers queueing at departures to drop off their luggage and collect boarding tickets, etc. How easy it would be, he thought, for just one of the holidaymaker's bags to be intercepted at the hotel, loaded with cocaine, taken to departures by the unsuspecting owner then airside by the baggage handlers. However, what then, he thought, how would an airside rip-off take place?

Cristobal slowly relocated outside to the entrance of departures, he needed to think. Sitting on a bench, away from the building, with his tool-bag beside him in the crepuscular light, he reached for a Fortuna Red and lit up. He was not one for smoking generally but it suited his cover.

For two weeks running now, they knew that Moreno and Ruiz were acting suspiciously with lobster pots in the early hours of Wednesday mornings.

He pondered, 'if that pot contained the drugs... then, when an innocent holidaymaker's vacation was over and they left their luggage in La Posada's safe room... Moreno could obtain access, secrete the cocaine and somehow mark the baggage for one of his associates in the airport... but how?

'An Ultra Violet marker would do it! So, a late afternoon flight on a Wednesday would be best; the tourists would leave their bags in the hotel's safe room after vacating their accommodation at, say ten or eleven o'clock in the morning, waiting for the transport at, maybe one o'clock in the afternoon. They would perhaps, have a little lunch before their journey, no need to reopen the luggage.

'So, the target would probably be a mature couple, rehearsed in their holiday travelling habits and unlikely to need to access their baggage and would not notice an extra kilo or so in weight.

'The journey from hotel to airport would be, probably sixty minutes, another hour to get to check-in, for a flight at, a window of: five o'clock earliest, seven o'clock at the latest.

'Alternatively,' he considered, 'Moreno might have an associate with security clearance, who takes the drugs directly airside then gets them to a baggage handler who finds suitable luggage?'

He preferred his first option, an innocent mule rather than a weak link in the chain, who, if caught, might cave in and roll over to questioning. Cristobal slapped his thigh, stood up and threw the nub-end to the floor where he screwed the sole of his shoe down on it in a very self-satisfied way.

*

(Sun 22/3/98)

Late the next day Cristobal was back at the airport in his familiar workaday guise, plus a grubby high visibility waistcoat.

Going through staff security unimpeded, he headed down towards the massive spaghetti of baggage conveyors in the outbound section. The sounds of machinery and aircraft were loud and he reached into his tool-bag for his ear defenders. He also located his clipboard and Sound Level Meter; his reason for being there, if he were to be asked, was to check on noise decibel levels.

He had visited airside a couple of times previously, once as a guest when the airport underwent a programme of expansion and again, in a supporting role to an accident investigation.

Wandering from station to station, zone to zone, familiarising himself with the vast layout, his plan was to inspect methodically the entire area. Inevitably, that would bring him into contact with the baggage-handlers. However, interaction with staff did not worry him; he looked busy but not hurried; intent but not prying, exchanging nods and brief waves with the workers who simply accepted his presence. Regularly glancing at the monitor screens, he noted that an aircraft was departing to Dusseldorf Germany, at 7.20pm.

Positioned near the conveyor bringing the luggage down to a train of waiting trailers he stopped and watched.

The bags began to arrive and two operatives scanned the bar-coded labels that had been threaded around the handles of the cases by the check-in staff.

They then loaded them from the conveyor to the trailers and off to the waiting aircraft. Cristobal noted that the scanners were hand-held and the workers could easily tape a small UV lamp to the device, play the light over another part of the luggage and locate their target.

'Wait a minute,' he mused whilst rubbing his stubble and moustache, 'I'm looking in the wrong place, there doesn't need to be a check here, the *destination* baggage control is the key! What we need to do is have a UV check immediately *after* check-in here, *before* any luggage gets into the system! Then we'd know. But why are the security staff not finding the drugs? Is there a check being made by a corrupt customs officer or is the cocaine disguised in such a way that it's invisible? We need to step lightly here.'

Walking away from the building, he meandered to his "thinking bench" outside.

'So...' he thought, '...at the destination airport there would be at least one crooked baggage handler and maybe one or two corrupt customs officers... The bags would be located as they came off the aircraft and onto retrievals, ready to go to the collection carrousels... The crooked customs people would open the luggage using their lock-picks, if necessary, do what would look like 'spot check', remove the drugs and close up the bags, very simple!'

*

(Mon 23/3/98)

Cristobal was sitting in his office in La Joya, he was now shaven (save for his moustache!) and back in uniform. He picked up the phone and called Juan Rodriguez at the airport.

'Señor, I know that it's short notice but I would like your help to set up an in-depth check at your incoming baggage X-ray at departures this Wednesday evening...'

'No, it would only be for one or two flights returning holidaymakers from one particular hotel...'

'Well, you and I would be there, if you're free, that would help with numbers, no need for extra staff...'

'Yes, that's right; the "international investigation"…'

'That's fantastic, thank you… oh, please can you arrange for a couple of UV lamps to be available?'

'Just a hunch…'

'Great, I'll see you in your office at 4.30pm.'

He leaned back in his chair and, with one hand behind the back of his head, he rubbed his moustache with the other.

Chapter 17 (Wed 25/3/98)

Cristobal arrived at the airport SVA offices at a quarter past four. He was wearing a dark suit and white shirt with no tie, the collar open, looking smart but not officious.

'Señor Rodriguez, it's a pleasure to see you rather than chatting on the phone, how are you?

'I'm fine thank you Señor Dorantes, I trust you are too. Right, what have you got?'

They shook hands and both sat down in comfy chairs in Rodriguez' office.

'Purely on a need-to-know basis, I would like this to stay between us two, certainly not to get back to the Commissioner under any circumstances, at least not for now,' Cristobal said flatly.

'Absolutely, I understand completely. He's an *archipámpano*!'

'A big-shot! I could not agree more! Now I'm sorry to say that I think that the cocaine smuggling ring we're all investigating, may be passing some of the drugs through the airport here,' said Cristobal coming straight to the point, 'I know that we've assumed the smuggling was mainly a maritime issue, however, this is what I believe. There's a hotel in Santa Maria being managed by one Miguel Moreno, do a quick search on your computer and list hotels in Algeciras as the principal port...'

Rodriguez rose, went over to his computer and typed in the details.

'Miguel Moreno son of Juan and Barbara Moreno, Hotel La Loma, Algeciras, yes I have him,' Rodriguez looked up at Cristobal who had walked over to the desk, 'has a degree in hospitality from Les Roches, Marbella, what about him? There's no criminal record... He's been travelling here regularly from the mainland for over five years... He now runs La Posada Hotel, Santa Maria.'

'Well,' said Cristobal, 'La Loma is a hotel primarily for merchant seamen and Moreno may have been recruited, either there or at University, by a drug runner, dealer or whoever and has worked his way up the ranks. Now, I don't have anything concrete at the moment, that's why I'd like us to run some checks today.'

'That's fine,' said Rodriguez, 'so this is the hunch you mentioned. What are we looking for?'

'I think that the drugs are concealed in an unsuspecting traveller's luggage – exactly how, I don't know, yet – the bag or bags may be marked, in some way, perhaps with a UV pen. They pass through your security, as there's nothing to raise your suspicions. Then, after reaching the destination airport, the bags are located, the drugs removed by corrupt staff and then the bags reunited with their owners waiting at the carrousel. What do you think?' Cristobal asked Rodriguez.

'Hmm, I see what you're saying, could be... a compromised customs officer at the other end though...' he looked doubtful, '...rare but not beyond possibility.' He conceded. 'All right, let's get down to airside check-in.'

Rodriguez discretely asked one of his officers to direct any luggage coming from hotels in Santa Maria down to the last three x-ray machines on the run. At the penultimate two of those posts, he asked each operative to pay attention to cases and bags coming directly from La Posada Hotel and to send them on to the last machine.

Producing two UV flashlights, he handed one to Cristobal. Locating themselves at the end of the run, Cristobal acted as though he were a casual observer, after all, this was Rodriguez' territory.

They had already checked the flights and knew that there were only two for holidaymakers from La Posada, one to The Netherlands and the other, a later flight, to Scotland. Amsterdam was Cristobal's favoured destination as Schiphol was a very busy airport, easier for an airside rip-off to be undertaken.

Twenty-five minutes later the bags started to arrive from Santa Maria. Although the flight was more or less full, there were only twenty-eight passengers from La Posada.

The Luggage started to filter down towards them and finally one came through to the last x-ray station. It was a large, heavy cumbersome suitcase and was bound with several straps with the owners name woven repeatedly along their lengths. Cristobal shook his head at Rodriguez who understood that this bag was an unlikely candidate.

Several similar cases came next, all bound or padlocked. Both men knew that seasoned travellers, with nothing to hide, would have quite plain luggage and not use locks but prefer to use cable-ties, for they would be less likely to suffer damage if they needed to be opened by security staff. They had been playing their UV torches all over each case, after they had exited the x-ray and so far had seen nothing to arouse suspicion.

Finally, a likely candidate arrived; mid-sized, dark brown, with some old battered NL stickers, the type seen on car registration plates, and a cable-tie across the zips. Rodriguez and Cristobal nodded to each other and they peered over the shoulder of the operator to see the x-ray screen. There was nothing remarkable to see but on exiting the machine, they took the case over to an inspection table nearby. In the light of their UV torches a very definite, hand written, "2/2" stood out on the underside between the wheels.

'That's "two of two", I'd say, there's another somewhere, either we've missed it or it's coming soon…' Cristobal remarked, 'look, let's try that one, it's very similar…'

It was a comparable size and condition to the other case but dark blue with ragged AFC AJAX stickers. Again, the x-ray screen showed nothing obvious but when they took the bag to the table and shone the UV light on it a handwritten "1/2" between the wheels stood out.

Rodriguez picked up the case, 'bring that one,' he said to Cristobal, as he opened a door to a small side room and entered. Closing the door behind them, they took the bags and placed them, on a table.

From his jacket, Rodriguez produced a small, narrow bladed screwdriver and proceeded to slip its tip into the locking tongues of the cable ties holding the zips together on both cases. The men took a case each and, side by side, carefully began to inspect them.

Rodriguez had the brown case, he looked at the hand-written luggage label; Yolanda Van Cleak. He opened the case completely; it contained dresses, blouses, a sun hat, sling-back shoes, toiletries, a bag of laundry, a white hand-towel in a sealed bag, small electrical items for travelling, a novel and a glossy magazine, etc. He felt all around inside the case for false panels but there was nothing.

91

The blue bag was obviously masculine and had almost identical contents, even down to a white hand-towel in a sealed bag, No hidden panels, nothing to arouse any suspicions. Cristobal looked at the luggage label; Hank Van Cleak.

'Well,' said Rodriguez, 'nothing to see here, the marks on the bottom of each suitcase could be for the Van Cleak's own reference.'

Cristobal was carefully examining the bagged towels. 'Why are these sealed? I know it's a common sport to steal towels from hotels but one in each case, both an airtight bag? And they feel heavy,' Cristobal looked at Rodriguez, 'please can you radio for a sniffer dog.'

Presently, a handler arrived with his small Spaniel, a lively but obedient dog. Cristobal picked an espadrille from the case and passed it to the handler who positioned it on the floor in front of the dog. Nothing, the dog had a quick sniff then simply ignored it. Next, Cristobal passed one of the towels, as it was placed on the floor, the dog circled in front of it, sniffing. Rodriguez picked a knob pin from the back of his lapel, lifted up the bag and at the corner, pierced a small hole in it. He then squeezed the bag slightly under the dogs' nose. The dog continued sniffing, and then he sat still, still snuffling and looking directly at the handler and Rodriguez as he held the bag. The handler passed a treat to the dog and began petting and praising him.

'He's normally a bit more demonstrative than that,' the handler noted, 'but that's positive.'

'Yes, convincing,' Rodriguez said, picking up the towel and examining it closely, 'thank you,' he said to the handler, 'well done, you can return to your station now.' Then, to Cristobal, 'so, you don't think we should pick up this Dutch couple, just repack the cases and send them on their way?'

'Yes, that's right,' Cristobal answered, 'I don't believe they're involved at all. I suggest you make careful contact with the authorities at Schiphol. Alert them to the situation and to intercept whoever is collecting the towels, at their convenience. I'll liaise with the EDU so that they're fully aware of what's going on and can collate all the intelligence we have, they'll instruct Schiphol accordingly.'

'I agree,' responded Rodriguez, 'so how have they got the cocaine in there? I can't see any powder residue and there doesn't seem to be another bag inside, the towels must be impregnated with it, don't you think?'

'Yes it looks like it,' said Cristobal, 'It's not too complicated, just a few chemicals, some knowledge and somewhere to work. Moreover, I think I may have that part of the puzzle already. Of course, because this system works for them, this particular flight may not be the only one each week, please be vigilant.'

They repacked the cases, zipped them up, replaced the cable-ties and then put both bags back onto the conveyor on their way to the aircraft.

'So your hunch was correct, you must be pleased.' Rodriguez said to Cristobal as they walked back to the office.

'Yes, we're a step closer to understanding what's going on, it's another layer of the onion... we just don't know how big the onion is!'

'Quite so, I'm a little annoyed that my staff hadn't picked this up though!' said Rodriguez.

'Don't be too hard on yourself, this may be a relatively new side of the operation, we just do not know. It's possible that the visits to the mainland that Moreno has been making, over the last few years, were ones where *he* was the mule. However, since he's been in Santa Maria, he's taken on an organisational role and developed this particular international strategy more recently. I know it goes against the grain and you would normally arrest anyone with drugs but in this case, given the size of the undertaking, the EDU will want you to let it pass. It's all about the 'big picture'. '

'I know, I agree entirely, and my orders are to give priority to the broad view.'

The two men shook hands and Rodriguez went to his office to begin his report for Schiphol.

Cristobal drove to La Joya to send his account to the EDU. He informed Alvaro of his findings the following morning.

Chapter 18 (Sat 28/3/98)

Cloud was tumbling over the mountaintops above Fernando's apartment and rain was beginning to obliterate the view of Santa Maria, when Cristobal and Alvaro arrived. The three men sat with coffee at the dining table that was strewn with paperwork.

'Huh,' said Cristobal indicating to the patio and balcony, 'I hope it's not like this next Saturday when we expect that boat to arrive! So, anything to report Fernando?'

'Nothing specific from the harbour,' said Fernando as he passed his observations over to Alvaro, 'but I did manage another trip out with Ruiz on his boat last week.' Addressing Cristobal he said, 'you were right about the satellite phone; it's a Motorola Iridium, I let Alvaro have the details during the week, also Ruiz has a lot of diving equipment, sorry no photos'.'

'Yes, he mentioned it to me, did you get on to it Alvaro?' asked Cristobal.

'I'm still waiting for the call logs from the satellite company; hopefully we'll have them this coming week.'

'Very good, now Fernando, tell me about the diving equipment,' asked Cristobal.

'Well, wetsuits, scuba tanks, masks, flippers, all the usual stuff but there was also a Farallon DPV...' Fernando described his afternoon at sea... 'Ruiz was not at all happy that I'd seen his gear but thankfully I'm sure that he accepted my naivety... I wouldn't want to get on the wrong side of him...'

'All right, here's what I think,' began Cristobal, rubbing his moustache, 'Ruiz is contacted by the gang at sea and is told where and when to meet. He collects the cocaine and secretes it in at least two places: Playa de los Chicos, using lobster pots, he has a licence for the whole bay, also he probably has a cache in those dangerous caves at Los Roques, that's why he needs specialist diving equipment. Maybe the drugs are hidden elsewhere too. Of course, it is possible that he dives on old wrecks...

'Anyway, on the days and times that we know about, thanks to Chris Baker, Ruiz brings the drugs to Santa Maria, where he conspires with Miguel Moreno and others.

'My investigations have shown that Ruiz is also involved in buying chemicals, which can be used to alter the cocaine's appearance. I'm now convinced that the process is taking place in the old offices under La Posada's swimming pool. The cocaine is impregnated into towels, which are then hidden in a tourists' luggage and shipped abroad via flights to The Netherlands and perhaps other destinations. I tested this successfully last Wednesday, with our Airport Security and, Bingo! I was right!'

He leaned forward and looked at the other two men fixedly, 'I've been instructed that we will be involved in a big sweep operation, soon. Fernando, you will need to make sure that your radio is fully charged as I'll be relying on you to feed information to us, from up here, on the day.'

'*Diablo*, when will this be?' Fernando asked incredulously.

'*Very* soon by the sound of it,' said Alvaro, 'I think that we should have some radio-operational nomenclature and make sure that Fernando's frequency is not one that could be picked up by anyone other than us, don't you think, Cristobal.'

'Absolutely yes! Let's see, Fernando you'll be *Foxtrot*, Alvaro; *Alpha* and I'll be *Charlie*.'

Cristobal leaned back in his chair, 'Alvaro, you can rely on three armed officers and I can only spare five for here; the rest of my people will be with other units elsewhere. Hopefully we'll outnumber the bastards but at least we'll have the back-up of the *Grupo Especial de Operaciones* – GEO,' he looked at Fernando who had visibly paled, 'they've been countering the ETA Basque Separatists but will be sent to us at short notice.'

'These smugglers, they're like rats!' pronounced Fernando, 'they keep themselves secret and quiet but all the while they're doing their dirty business right under our noses!'

'Good analogy,' said Cristobal, 'and just like rats; if they're cornered they'll scatter or fight to the death... we have to get this right first time. We have to get all of them in one go. I cannot stress the importance of this Fernando. We also have to assume that they can monitor all of the security services radio channels, which is why your role is so important.'

'Understood,' Alvaro nodded, 'well the lobster pots routine was repeated again, early on Wednesday morning but nothing else to report. Fernando, cast

95

your mind back to New Year's Day. How many men did you see on the harbour?'

'Er, two were in the van and two on the boat... Oh yes and the two who were already there, by the buildings and wondered over to the others by the van. Hmm, after off-loading the boat, four got into the van and the other two sailed off on the boat, which headed south. I didn't see where the van went but I did see it a month later, when it went up Calle García to those old offices...'

Cristobal responded, 'Okay, our intelligence suggests it's unlikely that there are any other people directly involved here, as these types of criminal usually work in their own small family-gang but we can't know for sure.

'Now, our part of this operation is purely land-based; the SVA will concentrate on every aspect airside and the Coast Guard and others will take care of everything out at sea. As I said, the GEO will back us all up and even I don't know what they will have in mind; *we* don't *need* to know.

'As I mentioned before Fernando, these smugglers are very dangerous, hardened criminals who will stop at nothing to get their own way and to survive. They will be armed and I'm quite sure they'll be ready to do whatever is necessary to avoid capture. This is not a game and you've been very helpful to the investigation and we're most grateful, but we still need you Fernando. However, other than being our eyes from up here, I don't want you to put yourself at any more risk.'

'I can't say I'm not relieved, but I'm very happy to help in any way that I can,' said Fernando, 'I never thought of Santa Maria as a hot-bed of low-life activity. To me it's a quiet back-water holiday resort; chilled-out and laid-back, as they say. I really do hope that you can catch them all, quietly and with as little disturbance to the locals and tourists as possible.'

'Well I certainly hope so too Fernando,' said Cristobal. 'When I get details of the plan, I'll assess the risks, but operations like this always pose problems, some of which will be beyond our control. Now, are you fully conversant with the operation of your radio?'

'I think so; my boys had some walkie-talkies when they were kids, it's much the same I think.' Fernando said as he reached into a side drawer to retrieve the device, charger and the instruction manual, which Alvaro had given to him some weeks before. 'Switch on and volume control here, the digital display shows the frequency, battery charge and the key symbol which means it's locked to a particular channel. The PTT is here, on the side, so push-to-talk and release when finished… oh, it doesn't have a "Roger beep", so I have to say "Roger" or "Over".'

'Quite right,' Alvaro affirmed, 'you're pretty clued up on technology, aren't you? Well done! Here, I'll set a channel specifically for our use. Keep it fully charged and to hand. As soon as we know when we're going in, we'll let you know by one means or another. How about a code word Cristobal… maybe; "Albatross"? Sounds suitably obscure and should transmit well.'

'Excellent plan, Alvaro. Fernando, these operations usually take place early mornings, but we'll give you as much notice as possible.'

'I'll be ready,' Fernando said, as stoically as he could. 'Oh yes, can I just draw your attention to that day when I saw the van drive up Calle García, on the 2nd February… There was a green lemonade tin, which was on the wall by where it happened… Then, four weeks later, on 3rd of this month when the boat didn't show up, there was a red cola tin in the same place… those are the only times that I've seen them. Maybe it's just a coincidence or a signal perhaps?'

'Right, yes I remember you saying…' Said Cristobal, smoothing his finger across his top lip, 'it is a bit tenuous but it could be a signal to Moreno and Ruiz's minions that the shipment is coming, or not. Alvaro, we're sure that a week today is the next delivery at 10a.m. Set up your surveillance camera vehicle to see if a green tin is placed on the wall. Best do it up from midday on Friday if possible.'

'Will do. Where exactly was it Fernando?' Alvaro asked.

'Just past Calle Lorca, on the right heading down to the marina, the wall is about 1.4 metres tall, dead opposite Calle García.'

'It's a bit awkward to park a vehicle there. I'll see if I can arrange for one of my men to watch in person for a few hours. It may take a couple of shifts though, posing as a tourist visiting the shops and bars, or something like that. Leave it with me.'

'Now remember gentlemen, the clocks go forward tonight from Western European Time to WET plus one, I know that it's Sunday tomorrow, but don't get caught out!' said Cristobal, with a wink.

Chapter 19 (Fri 3/4/98)

Cristobal had not been looking forward with having to bring Commissioner López up to date about the plans to arrest the smuggling gang in Santa Maria. On a need-to-know basis, López *needed* to be given the knowledge that Cristobal had and his visit was now overdue and urgent. However, the Santa Maria connection was only part of a bigger picture, for which Cristobal did not have all the information; his concern was only for his 'patch' and he didn't need to know any more than was necessary to fulfil his duties. He also wanted to inform López of a personal matter. So, it was with some trepidation that he approached López' office secretary.

'Good day Senorita,' he said, 'Chief Inspector Dorantes, I'm here to see the Commissioner.'

'Oh, I'm sorry Chief Inspector he's gone away with some friends for a few days playing golf. Can I help at all?'

Cristobal's anxiety turned instantly into infuriation, but he strove to keep it from the young woman in front of him.

'Oh, I see,' Cristobal said, 'I have a very important document here,' he produced an envelope from his pocket; 'I'd like to put it on his desk if I may. When do you expect him back?'

'Yes of course, go straight in, Commissioner López should be back on Monday or Tuesday.'

Cristobal thanked the secretary and went into the office, walked straight to López' chair and sat down. He drew a ballpoint from a choice of many in a container on the desk. On the front of the envelope he wrote in block capitals; 'FOR THE URGENT ATTENTION OF COMMISSIONER LÓPEZ', and propped it up in a prominent position. 'What an imbecile,' Cristobal thought.

*

Throughout the week, Fernando had been busy helping clients complete their *modelo* tax declaration forms, for submission after 6th April, which had helped pass the daytime hours. He had been restless all week and the continuing overcast weather had not helped.

99

It had been pointless trying to watch the harbour from his balcony as it was virtually invisible due to cloud and rain. The forecast was for the sky to clear overnight; he certainly hoped so as he wanted to be sure that he could note down the progress of *El Alborán*, if it really was to show up on the following morning.

By four o'clock Fernando had completed his work for the week and went out to Simon to tell him to finish too when there was a ring on the doorbell. They could see through the obscure glazing the shape of a uniformed figure standing in the corridor.

Fernando opened the door, 'Captain García, come in, what can I do for you?' he asked.

Alvaro offered his hand, which Fernando shook, 'Senor Fernández, a personal matter. Do you have a few minutes?'

'Yes of course.' Then directing his attention to his assistant said, 'Simon, I'll lock up, see you next week. Captain, please come into my office.'

Once inside Alvaro said, 'Right, here's what I can tell you; the EDU have told us to perform the raid tomorrow. Our operation is one of several. We're only concerned with Santa Maria, but it turns out that the drugs operation is bigger than Cristobal and I had been informed. It seems that Ruiz's boat is not the only one collecting the cocaine way out at sea, so there will be coordinated raids across the archipelago. We must concentrate on our part only. Ruiz should be arriving tomorrow at ten o'clock, as you know. Now, that's not ideal, as it's the weekend and there will be people about, but those are our instructions.

'It is vitally important that we need you to be scanning for *El Alborán* so that we can time things accurately. The coastguard will head the detention of the boat, after delivery, when it's left the harbour.

'Meanwhile, all our operatives will be stationed in and around La Posada ready to arrest the others when they arrive with the drugs in the van. Timing is crucial; this needs to be swift and decisive. We cannot afford any slip-ups. I don't need to stress the secrecy that we need to keep here Fernando. Now, for what it's worth, I have an officer watching the wall over the road, for a drinks tin to be placed, I'll let you know later if and when that happens. Any questions?'

Fernando could feel that his heart was pounding and his palms were sweating. He swallowed, 'where will you and Cristobal be?'

'Well I want to get Moreno, so I'll be in the hotel somewhere, it depends. Cristobal's station will be behind the bushes on the wall where the drinks tin should be. It's a good vantage point to see when the van is leaving the marina and driving up Calle García and he can coordinate from there.

'We think that the van will drive into the garage section of the offices and we do not want that. We need to stop it before it enters; if we can surround the van there will be less chance of a fight. Otherwise, if they gain access to the offices there could be a prolonged standoff and they might be very heavily armed.

'Although GEO know our strategy we don't know theirs. We assume that they'll turn up and take over if things go amiss. In addition, there will be a few *Police Local* about to try to keep the public safe.

'I had hoped that we could get a sniper on your balcony or another building but we don't have the manpower and I'm not sure it would serve a purpose. Fernando, we just can't plan for every eventuality; these operations rarely go without one problem or another, we just have to do our best.'

'I understand Alvaro, just try to stay safe. Meanwhile, let's hope that this cloud and rain clears and we can see literally, what's coming! I'll have an early start and radio through as soon as I have anything to tell you.'

'With good fortune we will prevail! We'll be in contact tomorrow,' responded Alvaro, as the two men shook hands again, '*Gracias* Fernando.'

PART 3

Chapter 20 (Sat 4/4/98)

Fernando had no need to set an alarm for he had been wakeful most of the night, so had arisen early to make a coffee and breakfast *bocadillo*. However, it did nothing to alleviate the hollow feeling in his stomach.

He walked out onto his balcony as the morning light showed that thankfully, the sky had cleared; it was completely free of cloud and the air felt cool and fresh. It would be a very bright day, quite a shock to the eyes after a week of rain and no sunshine. He wiped a small puddle from his favourite seat and set up the telescope to begin viewing the activity at sea.

The sound of the San Isidoro church bell chiming eight o'clock drifted up from the main square and mingled with the twittering of small garden birds.

Scanning the seascape, he could see several fishing boats, way out at sea, slowly plying their way back to land. Next, he looked at the harbour, where there was increasing activity as people readied themselves to land the catches. 'I do hope that they're all dispersed by ten o'clock!' he said quietly to himself.

Panning over to La Posada, he could see little activity around the gardens and he was disappointed that the hotel obscured his view of the parking area and offices below the main swimming pool.

Adjusting the magnification of the telescope, he attempted to view the top of the wall where the green drinks tin could be but bushes nearby prevented it. 'That's where Cristobal should be,' he thought.

Widening his field of view, he took in the whole scene before him. Then he focussed in on the lower end of the harbour, where he assumed that *El Alborán* would dock. He moved the telescope as if to follow the pale yellow van up, through the gates and then turn right into Calle García. That was when he saw them, two men walking down to the marina from Calle García... Fernando whispered to himself, 'That's them! They're the two, they were there on New Year's Day, I'm sure of it!' He felt queasy, perhaps it was adrenaline, maybe it was fear. The two men turned right at the marina and were hidden from view by the buildings there.

Sitting back in his chair, he took a deep breath after realising that he had been holding it in and then shivered although he was sweating.

103

He closed his eyes briefly and images of guns firing and innocent people screaming and running for cover... children crying for their parents... police bearing down on the criminals... explosions... '*Diablo*, pull yourself together, everything is under control, Cristobal and his team know what they're doing... don't they...?'

'How can I convey the presence of these two men in the marina to Cristobal and Alvaro?' he thought...

'Foxtrot to Charlie Alpha: two men where your Englishman was, over.' He hoped that they had their radios on and could understand his cryptic message.

'Charlie to Foxtrot Alpha, roger,' came back Cristobal's response.

'Alpha to Foxtrot Charlie, roger. And Foxtrot... green tin positive, over.' From Alvaro.

'Foxtrot, roger.'

Fernando reset the telescope to a wide field of view and looked for any other movements of people, which might indicate anything unusual. Specifically, could he see more police uniforms than normal? It took a couple of minutes and then he spotted two officers of the *Police Local* standing in the main square. There were another two by La Glorieta and a couple at the end of his own road, Los Pinos. There must be others, he thought, but they would be keeping a very low profile.

As for Alvaro's *Guardia Civil* and Cristobal's *Police Nacional*, until needed, they would be almost invisible. They just had to wait. But waiting was very uncomfortable for Fernando; it was not quite nine o'clock and the town was getting busier with tourists and the potential for a disastrous outcome was increasing by the minute. He turned his back on the balcony, went to his kitchen and made a fresh coffee.

On his return, queues were forming on the quayside as fishing boats came in and their catches were off-loaded. Many holidaymakers were busy buying tickets for whale and dolphin watching boats, whilst others were preparing for fishing trips.

Fernando expected that the press of people at the harbour, would reduce by ten o'clock, but would it be quiet enough? He hoped so and began scrutinizing the distant northern horizon and coastline for *El Alborán*.

Of course, he knew from recent experience that it would take about forty minutes for Ruiz to bring his vessel from near Playa de los Chicos to Santa Maria. Surely, he should be able to see it by a quarter past nine.

As time slipped by, Fernando became more and more restless. By half past nine he was beginning to panic, as there was no sign of *El Alborán*, but at least most of the harbour was less busy.

He began to doubt himself; conceivably the smugglers had wind of the operation; maybe the boat was not coming, perhaps his watch was wrong? 'Wait a minute… *Diablo*, they could still be working on Western European Time! We've assumed that they're on WET plus one, if so; they'll be coming in at eleven o'clock not ten!

Reaching for his radio he announced, 'Foxtrot to Charlie Alpha, Albatross negative, Albatross negative. Perhaps *not* W, E, T, plus one. Maybe W, E, T, zero. Repeat, maybe W, E, T, zero, over.'

After waiting for what seemed like minutes, but was only a few seconds his radio crackled and Cristobal came on, 'Charlie to Foxtrot… roger.'

The pressure was really getting to Fernando and he had to take himself off for a toilet break.

Back at his station, he methodically played the telescope over the townscape. The three pairs of *Police Local* were still at the locations where they had been before. It looked like two cars had collided at the junction just up from Calle García and both Police and passers-by were taking an interest. 'I wonder if that's a road block created by Cristobal,' thought Fernando.

Then he noticed a car was parking up Calle Juan Carlos. It looked just like Cristobal's, but an old man was getting out of it. He was wearing dark, baggy trousers, a tatty jacket and straw hat from which straggly grey hair bushed; he looked a little like Señor Arrabal! 'Ah, just a gardener,' thought Fernando.

People were going about their business as usual and, thankfully, the harbour was much less frenetic than it had been.

Adjusting the telescope zoom towards Playa de los Chicos, Fernando then looked slowly and carefully for any fishing boats. He checked the time, five minutes to ten, 'slowly now, concentrate…' he said to himself. The image in his eyepiece was unsteady so he let go from holding the instrument and the picture stabilised; his hands were shaking as he placed them on his thighs.

105

He remained hunched and unmoving, barely breathing for about fifteen minutes until his backache became unbearable. He stood up groaning and stretched his whole body, then sat down again and assumed his position. That was when he caught his first glimpse of a vessel; it was in the right place, it was about the right time, it had to be *El Alborán*! He felt the adrenaline pump through his body, 'wait now, I must be sure...'

Alvaro was sitting quietly in the small park below the main square. The placement of a green tin on the wall had been a sure sign that something was going to happen. When Fernando's call came about the two suspects in the harbour, Alvaro's senses were heightened.

His men were hiding in a van parked in Calle García, and some of Cristobal's men positioned covertly nearby. Other *Police Nacional* officers were in the harbour area and elsewhere and Cristobal would take up his position when he was ready.

For Alvaro, it took a few seconds for the message about the one-hour time difference to sink in; for a moment he thought that the boat should have been in at nine o'clock, then realised that eleven would be correct. Therefore, they all just had to wait.

When the order was to come through, his instructions were to make his way quickly to the front entrance of La Posada; at a brisk pace it would take less than a minute. He would need to locate Moreno immediately, but there was no way of knowing where he would be...

Fernando waited a few more minutes; he needed to resolve the image in the telescope sufficiently to determine that the boat that he was watching really was *El Alborán*. The colour, size and shape may have been sufficient, but he just wanted to see if there were any gulls following. By a quarter past ten, he was positive that the boat he could see was their target and he grabbed his radio.

'Foxtrot to Charlie Alpha, Albatross positive, Albatross positive, over.'

Cristobal and Alvaro responded in the affirmative.

Fernando continued to monitor the position of *El Alborán* and its course was bringing it directly southbound to Santa Maria.

Knowing that it would be about five minutes before *El Alborán* docked, he adjusted the telescope's focus to have a quick glance around the harbour, the on-going car crash up the road and to see if everything else was looking safe.

'*Diablo*, what is that old gardener doing where Cristobal should be?' he whispered to himself. 'He's pruning the bushes!' He could only see the man's back, but there was something familiar about him; so Fernando re-adjusted the zoom and managed to get a good look at the man's profile as he turned to look down to the harbour. 'I don't believe it! It *is* Cristobal! How did he get his stubble and moustache so grey? Well, he's hiding in plain sight, that's for sure!'

It was true; Cristobal's disguise was perfect, just an old man doing a bit of gardening. However, he could see down to the quayside where the boat would dock and most of the way up Calle García, from where they assumed the van would emerge. Then, after loading, it would retrace back to the old offices, when Cristobal would alert the authorities to spring the trap.

Mercifully, the whole marina was quiet as the boat came alongside and tied off to the quay. The pale primrose yellow Transit van had slowly driven out of Calle García, and then reversed down the length of the quayside to *El Alborán*.

Fernando was watching intently, barely daring to breathe, but his heart stopped when he saw a yacht slipping into the harbour mouth. He had been so intent upon *El Alborán* that he had been almost completely unaware of anything else. Now the progress of the small yacht took all of his attention; he prayed that it would stay well away from Ruiz and was thankful when it made for the fuel station on the opposite side of the marina.

He knew that Cristobal's perspective would mean he would be oblivious of this development, but it was not worth reporting anyway. In addition, Cristobal would be unable to see neither how many people were involved at *El Alborán*, nor when the van would be ready to make the return journey.

Fernando watched and waited. It appeared that the off-loading was nearing completion when he saw the two men stroll from the cover of the buildings and over to the boat, 'look-outs, I'd say, and extra muscle if they're needed!' There were six of them there, two from the boat, two from the Transit and the two on foot. They spent less than a minute chatting, but Fernando felt the impatience rising within himself, along with the adrenalin, which was coursing through his body.

He watched as two men boarded the boat and two climbed into the cab of the van. The others helped to cast-off, then one entered the back of the vehicle and the last man who then entered the cab, had closed the rear door.

El Alborán began to leave the quay and the Transit van moved gently forward.

'Foxtrot to Charlie Alpha, two on water, two on water, over.'

Both Alvaro and Cristobal came back with 'roger'.

'Foxtrot to Charlie Alpha, three up front one inside, three up front one inside. Now! Now! Over.'

'Charlie roger.'

'Alpha roger.'

The San Isidoro bell chimed eleven o'clock as Fernando watched the van make its way along the quayside towards the town. Cristobal looked like an old gardener who was trimming shrubs, but he was watching intently. Although the vehicle had no windows save for the cab, Cristobal was careful not to compromise his cover by overtly radioing instructions to his colleagues; the van may have had spyholes. He waited until it had taken the right turn into Calle García before ducking down to make the call. He then turned around, still on his haunches, looked straight up in Fernando's direction and knowing that he would be in Fernando's sight, gave a quick thumb-up signal to him.

Fernando was shocked at the speed of what happened next.

There were several massive flashes from behind La Posada, visible even in the bright morning light, followed by very loud explosions and smoke, then the sound of gunfire. Police sirens started blaring out from all over the town whilst everyone ran for cover, except the law enforcement personnel who all headed, from their various positions, to the hotel. Cristobal stayed at his station, but Fernando could see that he was busy on his main radio.

The smugglers in the van had been taken unawares, but were determined criminals; the 'flash-bangs', thrown by the Police, had gone off around them as they approached the old offices, but the driver had performed a handbrake turn. The rear doors had swung open and despite the fact that officers surrounded them, the felons took their chances.

One man exited from the cab whilst another five jumped from the back. Cristobal had heard the radio call that there were more targets than expected and he realised that the van must have contained others of whom they were unaware. Police and *Guardias* were in position behind other vehicles, the hotel gardens, pool, and the rocks going down to the sea.

As the Transit had driven up Calle García, Fernando noticed movement, up to his left, on the rooftop of La Posada. Leaning over the far parapet, there was a man with what looked like a gun that he was pointing down to the back of the hotel. Fernando trained the telescope on the man and zoomed–in.

'That's the hotel manager,' he said out loud and immediately picked up his radio There was no point in being cryptic now; 'Foxtrot to Charlie Alpha, hotel manager on hotel roof… repeat, hotel manager on hotel roof, over.'

It was all that Alvaro needed. He was already in the hotel reception area and quickly ran to the service stairs by the main elevators, 'Alpha to Foxtrot Charlie, I'm on it… Over'

He bounded up the steps two at a time. He would be quicker than the lift, but five storeys, even for a fit man like him would leave him gasping for breath at the top.

Up and up he went, passing house cleaners, domestics and tourists, cowering at each level. 'Stay here…,' he shouted to them, as he continued his relentless climb.

He could hear the gunfire even from within the centre of the building and as he neared the top, the sound of bursts from Moreno's Mini Uzi 9mm-automatic machine gun increased. At the top, Alvaro slowed, he could see that the access door was open and he needed to tread carefully.

Moreno had the officers pinned down from above; he had already hit two officers and was aiming for others when Alvaro emerged into the sunlight. It was bright, very bright and he squinted to see where Moreno was shooting from and failed to notice a discarded satellite dish, on which he stumbled.

Fernando watched, horrified, as Alvaro with his Beretta 92 pistol in hand stumbled, but he stayed upright. Moreno heard him and wheeled around releasing a burst from his Uzi. Fernando saw Alvaro fall face down to the ground, immediately followed by the '*brrrrrt*' sound from the gun. Moreno must have been sure that Alvaro was finished, for he turned back to fire, once again, at the officers below. But he was wrong; Alvaro was not dead, yet.

Fernando forgot all protocol and radioed, '*Diablo*, Alvaro's down! Alvaro's down! Over.'

'Charlie, roger,' Cristobal came back.

Fernando's telescope was still trained on the hotel rooftop and he watched in disbelief as Alvaro rose himself onto his elbows and with his pistol take aim at Moreno. It was as if time had been slowed down; there was a brief puff from Alvaro's gun, Moreno's head spurted bright red and he fell over the parapet, immediately came the '*pop*' from the Beretta and Alvaro fell forward, unmoving.

Cristobal had broken his cover, pushed between the bushes and stood on top of the wall where the drinks tin had been. He was about to jump down and run up Calle García but the gang's van came careening down the road straight towards him. He raised his pistol and aimed at the driver, but the passenger had seen him. Two shots, in quick succession from Cristobal's gun and one from the passenger were almost simultaneous, but Cristobal had stood stock-still and his aim was true, he hit both driver and passenger. Instantly the inside of the windscreen spattered with blood as both the driver and passenger slumped to their left. The driver had dragged the steering wheel left too, and his foot remained hard down on the accelerator. The shot from the passenger hit Cristobal's left triceps passing straight through the muscle of his upper arm and the force threw him to the ground. The van was now heading wildly straight down the harbour, crashing and with sparks flying; it scraped at increasing speed against the wall on its left. It hit the far end wall square on, whereupon it burst into flames with a great explosion.

'Cristobal,' cried Fernando, 'not you too…' Grabbing his keys, he fled as a man possessed, from his apartment down to his car and, with tyres screaming, raced near to the bottom of Calle los Pinos and abandoned it. To avoid the roadblock, he ran down the steps and passageways between the roads, through to Calle Juan Carlos and down to Calle Lorca, then as fast as he could to Cristobal. As he reached him, there came a great clatter as two military helicopters appeared from behind the hills to the East and hovered over the town.

'Cristobal, Cristobal,' Fernando shouted over the din as he ran to the wall.

'Over here,' came the reply from between the bushes.

Fernando mounted the wall, quickly located his friend and helped him out of the shrubbery.

Lines dropped from the choppers and GEO operatives were abseiling down to help secure the town.

Fernando was very shaken, '*Dios Mio*, I never thought I'd see anything like this...'

'I know, and I don't want to see any more of it either...' Cristobal said with a groan as he cradled his arm, 'now quickly, there, pass my radio, I'll call for a medic for Alvaro. Do you think he's okay?'

'I, I, I'm not sure... it didn't look good... but he got Moreno...' Fernando said, whilst pressing the PTT on the radio and held it for Cristobal to make the call. He gave his position.

The helicopters wheeled away to the South and all the noise abated except for the shouts of men from around the hotel and the persistent wail of sirens. At least the sound of gunfire had stopped.

Fernando quickly removed his shirt, leaving his T-shirt on, tore off a sleeve and tied it round Cristobal's arm to staunch the blood flow, then fashioned the rest of the garment into a makeshift sling.

'Can you stand Cristobal?'

'*Gracias amigo*, yes, it's just my arm...' he said through gritted teeth and they walked back to the main road and waiting ambulance. 'I'll be fine now Fernando, please go to see what you can find out about Alvaro.'

Fernando needed no more encouragement and gave an affirmative nod to Cristobal, turned and ran off to the front entrance of the hotel.

Police with loud hailers were demanding all people should stay indoors, so it was no surprise that Fernando was challenged, especially as he had Cristobal's blood on his T-shirt!

'HALT!' a *Guardia* shouted, pointing her weapon directly at Fernando; for all she knew he could have been one of the criminals.

111

Fernando stopped and raised his hands, 'I've just come from Chief Inspector Dorantes; he's been shot but wants to know how Captain García is…'

'Very well, approach; is that your blood or his?'

'His, he's been shot in the arm, I think he'll be all right, but how about Alvaro, I mean Captain García?'

The *Guardia* lowered her firearm, 'not good, they're bringing him down now…'

Fernando ran over to the hotel entrance. There were several medics surrounding a stretcher and were just about to put Alvaro into the waiting ambulance.

'Are you all right?' a medic asked Fernando, looking at his bloodstained clothes.

'Yes, I'm fine. It's not my blood…' how is the Captain, your patient?'

'Fernando…' Alvaro croaked weakly from the stretcher, 'I got the bastard!'

'Yes, *amigo*, I know, I saw it all, now save your strength and I'll find someone to get Isabella.'

Alvaro nodded weakly and was taken straight into the ambulance.

Fernando ran back to the *Guardia*, 'please can you radio for an officer to collect the Captain's wife, Isabella. You could get her to the hospital to meet him far quicker than I could.' The officer got onto it immediately.

Fernando turned his back on the scene and walked away. The sound of the blaring sirens was overwhelming and he knew that he needed to get back to his sanctuary. Thankfully, the roadblock had been cleared for the ambulances and security vehicles, which were all busy racing to and from the town. There was still a lot of commotion from the back of the hotel and he did not want to think of the carnage that must have taken place there.

Back in his apartment, Fernando wandered from room to room, as a man lost in his own house. He could not settle, even though he was more drained than when Paco's son had found him just out of Fuente Armarga.

His emotions had been ripped to shreds and he could not get the things that he had seen out of his head.

Finally, he sat down on his bed. He was shaking all over. It was all too much for him; now he missed Amanda more keenly than ever. He put his head in his hands and wept.

When he entered his office, Fernando was not at his best; he had neglected himself, drunk too much, not eaten enough and had an upset stomach as a result. The stress of the last few months had also taken its toll on him. Perhaps it was just him, or was there a quiet stillness hanging over the town? He was not sure, but Simon could see that his employer was not himself.

'Good morning, are you all right Fernando? Coffee?' He asked.

'Oh, erm, coffee, yes please. I'm okay thank you, still just a bit shaken from Saturday,' Fernando answered distractedly.

'You, the whole town and island! But what's this I heard from our neighbours... someone saw you with blood on your clothes after all that shooting stopped...?' Simon asked expectantly.

'Not my blood and nothing for you to be concerned about Simon, I was just helping a friend of mine who'd been caught up in it. I'll tell you about it, someday.'

Simon could see that he would get nothing else from his Boss and so he dropped the subject.

'What's on the agenda for this week Simon?'

'Well, not surprisingly, most meetings have been cancelled or postponed. I think it might take a while for things to settle back down,' he answered. 'Do you think that it's all over; this raid and shooting and everything?'

'Oh yes, I'm sure it's all over, but you're right; it will take a while. It might be worth closing for this week. What do you think?'

'Yes, probably a good idea Fernando. There's some correspondence for you to deal with, other than that, I'd be happy to take the time off.'

'Right, I'll see to the paperwork. If you could make sure that the diary is empty, we can call it a day and reconvene next Monday.'

Simon cancelled all the appointments and had left by eleven o'clock. Fernando had done all he could and was completely up to date by early afternoon.

He had tried several times to call the University Hospital in Puerto de la Torre, but the switchboard was, for the most part, engaged and when he did finally get through, they would not tell him anything. There was nothing for it; he would have to go in person to see how his friends were faring. However, he feared the worst for Alvaro.

*

Fernando's landline was ringing as he got to the door of his apartment; he raced in and grabbed the handset.

'*Diga me...* Cristobal, Cristobal, are you all right? How are you? How's Alvaro?' Fernando shouted insistently.

'Slow down *amigo*, I'm okay. Touch and go with Alvaro, I've just been to see him; Isabella hasn't left his bedside,' said Cristobal flatly.

'I've been trying to call the hospital, but when I did manage to get through they wouldn't give me any information. Can I come to see you?'

'Leave it until tomorrow *amigo*. Things are still a bit crazy here, come over in the afternoon, fourth floor. I'll tell the staff to expect you; they probably won't let you in otherwise.'

'Right, I'll be there at three o'clock. It's so good to know that you're all right Cristobal, I'll be praying for Alvaro.'

'We all are Fernando, we all are. I'll see you tomorrow.'

Knowing that at least one of his friends was doing well helped to settle Fernando's delicate state of mind. He really needed to see Cristobal in person to have a debriefing, however incomplete it might be. Had all the work that they had put in over the last three months been completely successful? How many people had died that day and were there any civilian casualties? Had Ruiz been arrested by the Coastguard, or others? There were so many questions that needed to be answered, so Fernando began a list; he knew that it would help to organise his thoughts.

It did help and he began to relax, a little, although he was still very anxious about Alvaro. He also set about having a top-to-bottom cleaning session of his apartment, which passed the time and tired him out. At least he slept better that night.

When Fernando walked down to the town, there was still a strong police presence around La Posada and the whole area was cordoned off. He tried to speak with one of the guards who immediately moved him on, but he did learn that all the hotel guests and staff had been evacuated. There was no chance he could go up Calle García but doubtless Cristobal would know what was happening, even though he was in the hospital.

A morbid curiosity took Fernando and he walked to the wall where the drinks tins had been and where Cristobal had lain in wait for the criminals. Of course there was nothing on the wall but Fernando could not help himself; he needed to stand where his friend had been shot, so he climbed the wall and into the shrubbery there. He looked around and could see what a perfect place it was for concealed viewing of the scene.

Paying attention to the immediate environment, he saw something incongruous on the ground; a radio! It was exactly like the one that Alvaro had given to him. 'Ah, either Cristobal dropped it by accident or he didn't want anyone else to know he had this,' he thought, as he slid it into his pocket. The next thing he found was a tatty straw hat with an old grey wig crudely sewn inside it. Fernando smiled and shook his head in admiration and disbelief. 'I'll reunite him with his hat but keep the radio at home,' he thought.

Fernando was always punctual and he stood at the desk of the fourth floor reception in the hospital at three o'clock prompt.

'Señor Fernández, visiting Chief Inspector Dorantes please.' Fernando announced.

'Ah yes, you're on the list, just down the corridor there, Room 438,' the receptionist indicated with a gesture. 'He should be going home today, but there's no one there to help him.'

'Thank you,' Fernando responded, 'Hmm... I may be able to help with that, I'll see how he feels.'

Room 438 was a nicely appointed private chamber with all the usual hospital accoutrements.

Cristobal, his left arm in a sling, was sitting in a chair looking out of the large window when Fernando arrived. The two men smiled and embraced, as best they could, despite Cristobal's wound. He was wearing hospital pyjamas, a bathrobe and slippers. His demeanour was bright, despite him looking a little pale.

'It's good to see you Cristobal. How are you and how's Alvaro?'

'I'm fine, *gracias*. Alvaro is still in critical care, but we can go to visit him, if you like. It will give Isabella a break.'

'That's great! Oh… I believe that this is yours…' said Fernando and produced the straw hat from a bag, 'and I have your radio at home too.'

'Hah! I hoped that you would go to look for them!' Cristobal stated with a smile and placed the hat with his grubby old bloodstained clothes on a side table. 'Now come, let's go to see Alvaro. You'll need to push me in that wheelchair, over there. There's nothing wrong with my legs, but the doctors and nurses say that I mustn't overexert myself!'

'Of course, I understand. How badly wounded is Alvaro?' asked Fernando as they made their way to the high dependency unit and intensive care.

'He took four bullets: one smashed the right side of his pelvis which they've patched up with metalwork; one has taken parts of both his small and large intestines, infection is the worry there; another took his left kidney, he should be able to manage with just one. However, most worrying is the one that has grazed his spine, as they're not sure if any fragments of bone and the general trauma may have damaged his spinal cord… Apart from his life, his mobility and continence are in the balance… Apparently, they're going to try to reduce his sedation today…'

They went in silence for the rest of the way.

A nurse provided the two men with gowns and masks and then went into Alvaro's room to tell Isabella that she could take a break.

Her face was visibly wan when she exited the room and removed her mask.

'Isabella,' Cristobal reached out to her, 'how is he, any change?'

'No, no change,' Isabella said, downcast and with tears in her eyes.

Fernando approached her and extended his arms; she accepted his embrace gratefully. 'Have a break my dear, we'll sit with him for a while,' he said sympathetically.

The room was dominated by the bed and polythene-covered electronic machinery. There were wires and tubes everywhere and all sorts of humming and beeping sounds coming from various monitor screens, portable apparatus and other equipment.

The two men took up stations on either side of the bed and looked at their friend. A sheet covered him to his chest and his arms were on top. There was a frame beneath the sheet keeping it from Alvaro's abdominal wounds. His face was of good colour but that was due to the drugs being administered via a drip and oxygen from the plastic mask over his nose and mouth.

'Alvaro,' said Cristobal bending down to speak quietly into his ear, 'it's Cristobal and Fernando is here too...'

Fernando leaned forward, 'Yes, I'm here *amigo.*'

There was no response.

'He may be able to hear us,' Cristobal said to Fernando.

'I know. Have you told him that you were wounded too?'

'No I haven't... Alvaro it's true; I took a bullet through my arm but I'll be fine. It'll wreak havoc with my golf swing though!'

A sort of muffled gurgle came from Alvaro's direction and he croaked weakly through his mask, 'You don't... play golf...'

Fernando shot a glance at Cristobal, 'I'll get Isabella...'

Cristobal pressed the emergency nurse-call button.

A commotion ensued as Fernando re-entered with Isabella, followed by two nurses and a doctor in quick succession. The staff began adjusting some of the equipment and Isabella cradled her husband's hand in hers as he looked up at her.

It was obviously too crowded in the room and Cristobal addressed the patient, 'Alvaro, we'll leave you in these good hands and be back tomorrow.' Fernando wiped away a tear as they left the room.

Just along the corridor, Fernando could see a bench by a window, which had views into a quiet leafy courtyard. He parked Cristobal's wheelchair alongside and sat down. In silence, the two men composed themselves.

'Well, I'd say that was a positive encounter,' said Fernando, 'don't you think?'

'Let's hope so, he's young and strong and has the love of a good woman, but he's still in danger; it's his Road to Calvary…' Cristobal stated frankly whilst rubbing his moustache.

They sat quietly together for a while, and then Fernando asked,' Cristobal, on Saturday, did you set up that car collision in order to block the roads?'

'Yes, of course. It was only supposed to be for a short while, but as we were wrong about the timing it went on for over an hour, as you know.' Cristobal continued, 'We had officers and cars stationed covertly all around town so that when I sent the order they would sound their sirens, and close in towards La Posada. The hope was that the noise and commotion would frighten the locals and tourists who would immediately head indoors; in the main, it was successful, as there were no civilian casualties.

'What we couldn't and didn't know was just how many criminals were involved. Your observations told us of just four men in the van, but as it turned out there were another four already inside and two more in the old offices, plus Moreno on the roof.

'I didn't see for myself, of course, but I've been told that it was a bloody mess: two of our men died and four were wounded apart from Alvaro and me. Of the eleven criminals there, of whom we know about, only the two from inside the offices survived. They gave up after they realised that there was no hope for them.

'Ruiz and his crony were intercepted and arrested at sea but they may have been able to get a warning off to other members of the gang who are not in our scope of investigation.

'Actually, I proposed to the EDU that we should wait until next month for the raid but they insisted that we should strike. Of course, we only played a small part in a bigger operation.'

'*Dios mio!*' Fernando exclaimed, 'Well, I'm glad now that I couldn't see what was happening behind the hotel... So who was responsible for the drinks tins on the wall?'

'The Harbour Master, Pablo Méndez. He wasn't directly involved in the smuggling but the gang needed him to be out of the way each time they made their delivery. So, knowing that his wife was infirm, they threatened her life if he didn't comply with their demands. She would come to no harm provided he placed empty drinks tins, as instructed, on the wall as a sign to the other gang members, so he was to stay away from the marina on the appointed days.'

'Well, I used to take my boys fishing with old Pablo I hadn't heard that that he was Harbour Master now. So what about you Cristobal, why the disguise?'

'Simple, nobody notices the everyday, a commonplace gardener in this case. Theoretically, I should have been in uniform... In addition, no one seems to notice when I don't shave so I rubbed a little oil onto my stubble and added some talc, and with old clothes and a scruffy hat, I could see without drawing attention to myself. Somewhat unorthodox I grant you, but that's the way I operate.'

Shifting in his wheelchair to look directly at Fernando, he said, 'You were right; your *mirador* above Playa de los Chicos was a sort of look-out post. Ruiz's crony stationed himself there, so that when Ruiz turned up with the drugs there were two of them to organise the packages; some stashed in lobster pots and the rest taken to the caves at Los Roques. The two of them seemed to be operating independently but worked together, if you see what I mean. So it *is* possible that there are still some other members of the gang out there, somewhere... We don't know yet, we may never know.'

'So this still may not be over?' Fernando asked in shock.

'It's totally over as far as I'm concerned! In any case, it could be years before they can re-group and probably not here anyway.'

Fernando relaxed a little, 'So what exactly was going on in those old offices?'

'Well it's all still being investigated but they had a very sophisticated operation going on in there. They could drive their van inside and turn it around, the space is that large! They could store all the chemicals and other raw materials that were needed. They had tapped into the hotel electricity and water supplies, plus sewerage system for their waste products. They had a veritable production line going on! I'm sure that Moreno was the king-pin here; at some point in his life he was drawn into the international operation, but we'll probably never know when, or by whom...'

'Fair enough,' Fernando breathed a sigh of relief, 'now look Cristobal, the nurse said that you can go home today... how would you like to come back to recuperate in my apartment for a few days? I'd be honoured to have you and welcome your company.'

'That's very kind of you Fernando; yes, I'd like that, *gracias*. We'll have to call at my house, on the way for some clothes, toothbrush and razor, if that's okay? I can't live in my old gardening gear or this bathrobe!'

'No problem,' Fernando said with a smile.

As they approached Room 438 a nurse came up to them, 'Chief Inspector, you have a visitor...'

Fernando wheeled Cristobal into the room whereupon they were confronted by Commissioner López.

'Where the hell have you been Dorantes?' López demanded, addressing Cristobal directly who stood up, cradling his left arm in his right.

'Ah, Commissioner López, we've been visiting Captain García if you must know. Allow me to introduce Señor Fern...'

'I'm not fucking interested Dorantes. I want to know why so many people died on Saturday, I'm holding you personally responsible, you know.' López' anger was palpable.

Cristobal could feel the Commissioner's breath on his face, 'Commissioner, in operations like this there are always things that are beyond control of even the best organised...'

'And you were out of uniform!' López shouted, I think I'll have you demoted.'

'Well, I can't see how you can demote someone who has resigned!'

'What?' Lopez fumed, leaning forward staring directly in Cristobal's eyes.

121

Cristobal held his gaze and firmly pronounced, 'I visited your office last Friday in order to brief you about the operation which you *knew* was set for Saturday and also to give you my written resignation. Where were you? Off playing golf! And you obviously haven't been back yet, otherwise, you would have seen my resignation letter propped up on your desk! Now I'd call that dereliction of duty and I'll see that you don't work in public office here, or anywhere else in our archipelago, ever again. Now, *get out*!' Cristobal barked with a strength and presence that belied his stature.

Lopez was stunned but knew that he had been vanquished and, downcast, quietly left the room.

'Well, that felt good! As you've probably guessed Fernando, Commissioner López and I never really saw eye-to-eye, until now!' Cristobal said with a grin. 'I'll get changed into these old clothes, the staff will sign me out and we can be on our way.'

Chapter 23 (Wed 8/Apr/98)

After breakfast, Fernando drove Cristobal to his office in La Joya. Although technically he was still on sick leave, he needed to begin his report on the raid. As the two men entered, they met with a round of applause from Cristobal's colleagues who crowded round, which showed the great respect their superior commanded.

Cristobal thanked them all and announced, 'I'd like to introduce my dear friend and special adviser Fernando Fernández; he has been invaluable to me over the last few years and has helped considerably this year.' There were more brief sounds of approval from the officers.

'And today I'm his chauffeur!' Fernando quipped, which invoked some laughter.

Asking after Cristobal's health and showing their sadness at the loss of their comrades, an impromptu debriefing took place.

Finally, operational discussions were over and Cristobal told his colleagues that he was retiring from the Force. Whereupon muffled grumblings ran around the room and one officer muttered something about 'big shoes to fill', and another kidded, 'that's a tall order,' which induced a few sniggers.

'Very droll!' Cristobal smiled, 'Well folks, it's not up to me to decide my replacement; that's The Commissioner's job... firstly, they'll have to appoint someone to *that* position... we may all have to wait a while... In the meantime, I'm going to be around for the next three to six months at least. Now, if someone can organize a suitable tribute to our fallen comrades, that would be good, and please think of something for their families... Give it some thought people. In the meantime, it's business as usual, so back to work. We all have our reports to make and our normal duties to fulfil.'

Everyone made positive sounds and went back to their jobs.

*

The two men were at the hospital by early afternoon, for Cristobal had to have his wound checked and dressing changed. As soon as they were able, they quickly made for Alvaro's bedside. A telephone call which Cristobal had made earlier in the day only confirmed that Alvaro had had a comfortable night.

Having donned gowns and masks, they entered the room. Isabella looked up, her eyes were clear and bright, which immediately relaxed Cristobal and Fernando.

'How's the patient?' Cristobal asked, approaching the bed.

'I'm alive,' was the weak, but clear response from Alvaro. 'How's your golf swing?' A frail smile played on his lips.

'Hah! Don't you worry about that, you must concentrate on your recovery; you're needed back in your office!' Cristobal teased.

'Give me a couple of days… I'll be as fit as a flea!' he joked. 'Isabella, I need to have a chat with Cristobal and Fernando about Saturday's operation and I suspect you'll find some of what we'll discuss rather graphic. Please, go and take a break, I'll be fine.'

'Very well *amorcito*,' she said and lent forward to kiss his brow, 'I'll be back in a while.'

Cristobal rubbed his moustache and began, 'So how are you Alvaro, how do you feel?'

'Well, lucky to have survived.' Alvaro said feebly, 'But the long-term prognosis is somewhat blurred. I feel extremely fatigued, I have abdominal pain so I don't want to move, I have a catheter, an ileostomy and my legs feel strange with sort of shooting pins and needles. On the plus side, the morphine is helping but I've told the doctor that I don't want any more.'

Fernando manoeuvred a spare chair to the one side of the bed so that he and Cristobal could be sitting together as they spoke with Alvaro. They recounted their perspectives of the events of Saturday 4th, which helped each of them have a clearer understanding of what had transpired.

'Cristobal, I don't know what happened to my radio although it may have been recovered. You'd better check…' Alvaro said.

'Okay, I'll do that. It is possible that it has already been collected and assumed that it belonged to Moreno. I want to get onto the roof of the hotel anyway, so if it *is* still there, I'll find it.'

'I have to say Alvaro,' began Fernando, 'I really thought that you were finished. I've never seen anything like it nor been involved in such an episode before…' he then addressed both men, 'and whilst helping the two of you with your work has had its rewards, I really don't think that I am cut out for this line of activity!'

'Nobody is *amigo*, but we've been trained over many years and you've been more or less thrown into the deep-end!' Cristobal said with a gentle smile. 'We are very proud of you, *gracias*.'

Fernando smiled back at both of them as the door opened and Isabella re-entered with a doctor.

'Right, I think that's enough gentlemen. We don't want to tire the Captain too much,' the doctor said.

Fernando and Cristobal did not need to be told twice, as the health of their friend was paramount, so they took their leave and promised to be back soon.

Chapter 24 (Wed 15/Apr/98)

Santa Maria, although still quiet, save for the media crews, was beginning to show signs of normality; La Posada had reopened and all traces of the bloodshed had been literally washed away.

The harbour wall would always bear the mutilations of the van's progress before it crashed and the fire that had engulfed it.

The incident had made national news and although other raids took place elsewhere around the archipelago, Santa Maria had been the centre of attention. It was the main hub for the smugglers and where the hardest battle had been fought. Of course, things would never be the same again; the memories would fade, but still leave some physical and mental scars in the collective memory of the town.

*

A week of recuperation with Fernando and Cristobal felt able enough to cope in his own home. Alvaro was also showing positive signs of recovery and was out of intensive care. However, Fernando was still finding things difficult; his dreams were tormented and he resolved to get some counselling. After all, months of planning and information gathering had culminated in a frenzied few heartbeats of activity that had been over in an instant. He simply could not reconcile any of his tattered emotions.

Back at work, he found it difficult to concentrate. He had been in a routine of surveillance every morning for many weeks and that had stopped. He had been living a sort of double life that involved necessary secrecy and that too had stopped. In a perverse way, he was missing it and he knew that his life had changed forever. Perhaps he was bored?

'Simon, how do you feel about closing for a week next month?' Fernando asked his assistant.

'Another? We had last week off, remember?'

'Yes, I know but I have to say that I am feeling pretty jaded and think that I could do with going away for a few days… What do you think?'

'Well, to be honest Fernando, I agree that you seem very lack-lustre and you've not really been yourself all year for that matter, so yes, I think that a break away would do you good. What are the dates were you are thinking of? Where do you fancy going?' Simon asked as he opened his desk diary.

'Luis Miguel is playing *Plaza de Toros de la Malagueta* in Malaga on Friday 8th May and I have some friends up near the village of *Pastelero* who are big fans of his... If I can get tickets I'm sure they'd want to go and if there are none available I could still have a few days with them in *el campo* anyway, it may be just what I need...' Fernando said.

'So, close from Monday 4th open again the following week?' Simon asked, 'Yes I'm sure we can reschedule everything. There is a new client though, Paco Martín from, erm... Fuente Armarga, booked to see you on Tuesday 5th at eleven o'clock. Do you want to call him yourself?'

'Oh yes, I think I should as he is new, but I'm sure he'll understand. I need to allow enough time to take him to lunch as well. I'll call him now.'

Paco recognised Fernando's need of a short holiday, 'That's no problem at all, I visit my seafood suppliers regularly and I'll just fit in with you. Anyway another week before I see you can't make much difference! On another matter, of course we all saw the reports of the events in Santa Maria and there has been a bit of activity here recently too, since your visit... Some uniformed men trekking down to Playa de los Chicos... Is there a connection?' Paco asked.

'Erm... well... sort of... let's just say that the whole business has shaken me up, that's why I need to have a break away.' Fernando said.

'Okay, well I look forward to seeing you on the twelfth... Hah! That reminds me of a saying my grandmother had, "a holiday may help, but you'll still be taking yourself with you"...'

'Very true,' Fernando said, 'very true, your grandmother was a wise woman. Hopefully I'll be refreshed by the time we meet.'

Chapter 25 (Mon 4/May/98)

Cristobal's wound was healing well but Fernando still drove them both regularly up to Puerto de la Torre in order to see Alvaro.

They were all relieved when the doctors announced that Alvaro was improving so well that he would be transported to the smaller hospital in La Joya. It was good news all round; Alvaro no longer had a catheter and the surgeons were sure that his ileostomy could be reversed and, although there was weakness in his legs, his mobility was looking promising.

Both Cristobal and Isabella could get local transport to the new hospital. For Fernando it bought back memories of all the visits to that hospital that he had made for Amanda's treatment; a gloom still hung over him. He really was looking forward to his holiday.

*

Fernando had not been able to secure three tickets for Luis Miguel; they had sold out long before and even though there were cancellations, they were either single seats or only two together. Nevertheless, a break away and to see his old friends, Carlos and Bianca, in *Pastelero* would suffice, he hoped.

There was no need to take much; he could get all that he required into his hand luggage, but he began packing days in advance of his flight, although he still went by the adage of "take double the money and half the clothes".

He was excited, but not like he used to be before a holiday; his life was very different now from when he last went away. In fact, when he thought of it, he had not had a proper holiday for many years; not since before Amanda had died. Many months ago he'd told himself, when he moved from La Joya to his apartment in Santa Maria, that *a change is as good as a rest* and maybe that's true, in the short term, he thought.

*

A quick two and a half hour flight and Fernando was in arrivals at Malaga airport, embracing his old friends.

Carlos had spent time with the *Policía local* in Antequera but taken early retirement to concentrate on his hobby of giving guided walking tours of the mountains to tourists. Bianca was a retired psychiatric nurse who spent some of her time now helping at the local real estate agent's office.

As the three of them drove up to the village, they exchanged pleasantries and chatted in general. Carlos and Bianca brought Fernando up to date with all the local gossip and within the hour, they were crossing the threshold into their *finca, Casa Rosa*.

'Come in Fernando,' Bianca beckoned, 'your room is ready, get settled in and then come down to the terrace and we can catch up properly.'

'I'd forgotten just how stupendous your views are from here!' Fernando said, walking to the edge of the terrace and taking in the bucolic vista of fields, mountains and distant Costa del Sol. 'Mine are better though!' he said teasing his hosts with a wink. He stood for a while before sitting with his old friends beneath their sunshade.

From the 'fridge in their outside kitchen, Carlos had produced three bottles of ice cold *Mahou*, after all it was past five o'clock!

'So, Fernando,' began Carlos, 'it is *really* good to see you! Now, we haven't seen you since Amanda's funeral and given what's been on the television about Santa Maria recently, we assume that your visit now is not a coincidence...' he said, coming straight to the point.

'I suppose you're right.' Fernando said glancing at his friends. 'I've immersed myself in work since Amanda... to the exclusion of everything else... I think that it has been my way of grieving but it has not helped. Then this year, everything changed on New Year's Day...'

'Oh, *dear* Fernando,' said Bianca, 'you're carrying a weight, we can see that; you look pale and careworn, please unburden yourself and tell us your tale.'

'Very well,' Fernando conceded, 'but it might take a while...'

'Take all the time you want,' said Carlos. 'We're not going anywhere.'

Fernando began his story from Amanda's funeral, continuing to his move of office and home and then to having breakfast on his balcony on 1st January.

Details of the proceedings leading up to the current time he related clearly and left out nothing. His chosen profession helped him to recall the progression of events clearly and he was able to recount every detail. Another couple of beers during his narrative helped his animation and eloquence.

'That's an incredible story Fernando,' Carlos remarked, 'hardly believable but we know it's true and to have happened to *you*! I think that you have been out of your depth; your experiences are something that *I* might have relished given *my* training but not you! You never really were cut out for police work anyway. Right I'm going to prep' a meal.' With that, he lit his barbeque ready for chicken kebabs and began making a mixed salad.

Bianca and Fernando watched the last dying rays as the sun set beyond the distant mountains.

'I think that you have actually enjoyed your role in these events,' Bianca addressed Fernando, 'but Carlos is right; you've been totally ill-equipped to deal with the aftermath. Look at it this way; you've been in a rut since Amanda died, although you may still not recognise that, so when you realised that you could help with your friend Cristobal's investigation, you unconsciously jumped at the chance; it became a sort of hobby. On the plus side, it has helped you get physically fitter, but at the expense of your mental well-being. Over the next couple of days, let's dip in and out of analysing your position and get this jigsaw of emotions of yours sorted into a comprehensive picture. What do you think?'

'Oh yes please Bianca, that sounds good,' Fernando said emotionally.

'Fernando, bear in mind that we may not find all the pieces; there still may be some gaps for *you* to fill in…'

Chapter 26 (Sun 10/May/98)

At Carlos' suggestion, Fernando had started to write down his experiences of the last four months, mainly as bullet-points rather than diving into the detail.

Bianca's gentle probing was starting to have a beneficial effect; helping him to open up about his emotions and he was beginning to feel better.

Between them, they all agreed that Fernando should find some sort of hobby; keep fit, art classes, improving his English Language, anything to get him out to meet new people. It was one of the blank jigsaw pieces that only he could determine, but Bianca knew that there were others.

Many hours spent with Carlos out walking the hills had also served to blow away some of the cobwebs from Fernando's mind.

Carlos had deliberately taken him to various high points with fabulous views, also to hidden wooded valleys with trickling streams. They had observed the huge Griffon Vultures floating through the sky near *El Torcal*, watched the early migrating Bee Eaters wheeling and calling and they saw a Golden Oriole. They had even found some Lynx pawmarks in soft mud by a stream near *Sierra Blanquilla*. It was a world away from Fernando's normal life and he became stronger by the day; this new clarity and the perspective of his thoughts would serve him well in the coming weeks.

Promises to remain in contact with Carlos and Bianca, hugs, kisses and goodbyes said, Fernando boarded the flight home looking and feeling much improved. He now had a clearer understanding of what had befallen him in the past and could forge ahead into the future with renewed vigour.

*

His first action, when entering his apartment was to get on his landline to call Cristobal. They had not spoken for a week and Fernando was anxious to know how his friends were progressing.

'Fernando, great to hear from you,' Cristobal answered Fernando's enquiry. 'My 'golf swing? It is improving daily! How was your holiday, are you rested?'

'Very much so *gracias,* but no more adventures for me! How is Alvaro, can we go to visit him?'

'Yes, I was planning on going this evening. Is that convenient for you?'

'I'm on my way!'

Fernando was pleased to see that Cristobal was no longer wearing a sling, but could see how he was carrying his arm defensively. He was also delighted to see that Alvaro was out of bed and sitting in a wheelchair. He actually looked a picture of health, but that belied his condition.

In response to Fernando's questions Alvaro answered, 'Well, thankfully I'm on solid food. They've had me on my feet, just to see if I could stand. It was hard work and painful, nevertheless a step in the right direction, forgive the pun, and they're going to start physiotherapy. Oh and everyone here calls me "Chief Ironside"!'

'Huh, that's better than you calling me "Seve Ballesteros"!' Cristobal grunted.

'*Diablo*, what nickname do you have for me?

Cristobal looked at Alvaro then to Fernando, 'you're "the eye in the sky", but that is a bit of a mouthful... how about "Crow's Nest", that's where you've been advising us from.'

'Perfect.' Alvaro said.

'I'll take that, but I will always think of us as "The Three Witches"!' Fernando joked.

Chapter 27 (Tues 12/May/98)

Paco arrived at Fernando's office at eleven o'clock prompt. The two men exchanged all the usual greetings, settled down in Fernando's office armchairs and Simon placed coffees on the table before them.

'So it seems that you may have a tale to tell Fernando…' Paco stated bluntly.

'Well I wouldn't go that far Paco… let's just say that the authorities were able to act on some information, which I supplied…, perhaps I'll tell you more at a later date, meanwhile let's get down to business.'

Paco looked askance at Fernando, 'Absolutely, business before gossip!'

Having sold most of his shares in ITV Construction, Paco had a quite sizeable pot of funds on which Fernando could capitalise. They discussed bonds, stocks, pensions and other savings opportunities and decided on a mixed portfolio of investments.

An hour and a half later Paco asked, 'So how do you want me to get the money to you?'

'I don't mind; you could ask your bank to transfer it or write a cheque, it's up to you. What I cannot do is take cash! If you could sign the contract here and here please,' Fernando said, indicating, 'there are copies for you too.'

Paco wrote out a cheque, 'That's a lot of zeros after Pesetas, do you think that the talk of a European-wide currency will happen?'

'I think that it's inevitable as the Union grows. *Gracias* Paco,' said Fernando as Paco passed the documents, 'now, how about lunch? We can get a *menu del dia* at a little bar around the corner called *La Casa del Perro,* but that might be a bit too much like your own establishment! Or we could go to a restaurant, say *Casa Romero*?'

'I'd be happy at either, but as you say, a *menu del dia* would be a bit like having a day off in my own bar, so *Casa Romero* sounds good. Now I must make a quick phone call, if that's okay?' Paco asked, as he took out his mobile phone. 'Huh, no signal!'

'Here, use my landline. Do you have the number you want to call?'

'Yes, it's here in my contacts…' Paco dialled the number, '*Hola*, yes it's Paco. Can you meet us at *Casa Romero* in Santa Maria in half an hour?

Great, see you then.' He passed the handset back to Fernando who looked puzzled. 'Sorry Fernando, there's someone whom I would like to introduce you to, if you could give some basic advice in a relaxed venue, I think that it might be beneficial to both parties...' Paco said ambiguously.

'That's fine Paco, no problem. I'm intrigued.'

The two men strolled slowly round to the restaurant and were perusing the menu when Paco asked casually, 'Did you know that my older sister was widowed a few years ago?'

'No, oh dear how terrible, I'm very sorry to hear that Paco. I didn't even know that you had a sister.'

'Yes, she's had a really hard time. Her husband died tragically in a car crash but he did leave her and their daughter quite well off... You may know her anyway; she owns the Flamenco Dance Academy in la Joya? Anyway, I think that she would benefit from meeting you casually, in advance of a more formal consultation.'

'Oh, right that's no problem. No, there's no reason I should know her, after all Flamenco is not in my usual sphere of interest.'

'She teaches all Latin dance styles as well. Ah, here she comes now...' said Paco rising to his feet.

Fernando had had his back to the door and when he stood and turned around, he was greeted with the sight of a woman with long black hair. She was wearing blue jeans and a white T-shirt. She walked with an elegant gait, which he found both alluring and attractive.

Paco waved to her as she walked over to them. He reached out and they kissed on both cheeks in the customary manner, then he made the introduction, 'Mercedes, Fernando...'

Fernando reached out with both palms upwards and looked into her beautiful hazel eyes.

Mercedes placed her hands on his and looked directly into his dark eyes.

'It's you...' they both said in unison smiling at each other. It was like the curtains had been drawn back and the windows flung wide open on a sunny springtime morning; light flooded into their lives and new possibilities abounded.

Paco looked at them both and smiled.

Chapter 28 (Summer 1998)

Mercedes and Fernando had quite a lot in common, apart from both having been widowed; they enjoyed similar music styles, a love of nature and they were both considerate and compassionate. More importantly, they were mutually right and ready for each other.

However, Mercedes had no knowledge of wealth management and Fernando knew nothing about flamenco or Latin dance, so they had things to learn reciprocally.

'Stand up straight,' Mercedes commanded Fernando, 'head up, feet slightly apart, bend at your knees a little.'

'Ahh, that's uncomfortable,' Fernando complained.

'I know, now twist on the balls of your feet, about forty-five degrees to the left, but keep your body facing me, perfect. See how your left foot is a little further forward than your right? Now I'll mirror you and we can get into tango hold. Yes that's good, right hand into the square of my back now hold my right hand with your left, pointing ahead down the room, excellent. Look, between us, we have a V-shape in promenade position, remember that and try to keep it in mind.'

'*Diablo,* it's so unnatural!'

'Okay, were going forward three steps, head facing along your left arm then a quick "snap". So let's do that slowly, with your left foot, one, two, three. Now we're going to keep our bodies facing forward but you are going to quickly turn your head right and back, that's the "snap". Watch us in the mirror as we do it, follow my lead and we'll go again with the three steps, and do the whole thing.'

'Ah… I think I've got it.'

'Excellent!'

'But I'd rather go for a walk… or tuna fishing…'

'I'll make a dancer of you yet, you're picking it up quicker than most of my students! With your height, you'll always look elegant, but I *am* looking forward to teaching you the rumba; the dance of love…' she said and winked at him, 'but it's not easy to get right… and don't forget the Argentine tango!'

'Well I'm looking forward to teaching you about the stock markets and off-shore investing!'

'One thing at a time, right let's try those steps again.'

*

In August, Miguel and Pablo managed to get time off together and they arranged a vacation with their father. It was a perfect opportunity for him to introduce Mercedes and her daughter Emilia and they all got on well.

For the three weeks that the boys had, the two families flitted between Mercedes' villa in La Joya and Fernando's penthouse. They all went out on little day trips, short walks, visited Cristobal, Alvaro and Isabella and met with some of Mercedes' close friends.

Fernando explained to Mercedes, Emilia and his boys what had been going on over the first five months of the year, but kept much of the detail to himself. After all, his involvement with the raid was purely on a need to know basis and they did not *need* to know, not yet anyway.

*

Cristobal finally finished work in September to great fanfare from his colleagues. Retirement was an opportunity to attempt playing golf, but learning how not to slice the ball was an issue. Nevertheless, he began to enjoy it, if only for the fresh air walking! However, as he was always in demand as a consultant, by the police forces, for his expertise in crime fighting, so he kept busy.

Alvaro's recovery was steady and by the time he was ready to go back to work, everyone was pleased to see him elevated to the position of Commissioner. Although the moniker of "Chief Ironside" irked him slightly, the genuine use of it by his team members touched him. At least, unlike his namesake, he only relied upon a walking stick for mobility, for which he was grateful.

Chapter 29 (Thurs 31/Dec/98)

Emilia was with college friends but Mercedes stayed over with Fernando for New Year's Eve. They sat on his balcony waiting for the impressive annual firework display at the harbour and headland, as the San Isidoro bell chimed midnight.

'Happy New Year, here's to absent friends.' They said together as they toasted each other.

To himself, Fernando also raised his glass to the acknowledgement of a most extraordinary twelve months. What would the following year bring? He wondered, as it would be the last one of the century *and* millennium.

Glancing across to Mercedes, he saw that she was looking at him with her beautiful hazel eyes.

'What are you thinking?' She asked softly.

'Oh, I'm thinking that despite the trauma of the first half of this year, the second half has been a tranquil balm, I'm glad that Paco introduced us; I feel blessed.'

'*Igualmente amorcito*, likewise sweetheart.'

From the vantage point of the crow's nest, they held hands and watched as the fabulous pyrotechnics lit up the night sky before them, the herald of a new year and a new foundation.

* * *